A Caring Errand 2

A Strategic Reading System for Content-Area
Teachers and Future Teachers

DR. DONALD J. YOKITIS

Copyright © 2022 Dr. Donald J. Yokitis
All rights reserved
First Edition

PAGE PUBLISHING
Conneaut Lake, PA

First originally published by Page Publishing 2022

ISBN 978-1-6624-7695-2 (pbk)
ISBN 978-1-6624-7696-9 (digital)

Printed in the United States of America

Applied
Dissertation

EdD Program in Child and Youth Studies

Nova Southeastern University
Fischler School of Education and Human Services
Applied Research Center
1750 NE 167th Street
North Miami Beach, Florida 33162-3017

Reading Instruction in a Content-Area Course
Enhancing Secondary Students' Reading Achievement

by
Donald Yokitis

An Applied Dissertation Submitted to the Fischler School of Education and Human Services
in Partial Fulfillment of the Requirements for the Degree of Doctor of Education

Nova Southeastern University
2006

CONTENTS

Preface 7
Acknowledgments 9

Chapter 1: Introduction 11
    Statement of the Problem 11
    Purpose of the Project 13
    Research Question 14
    Definition of Terms 14

Chapter 2: Review of the Related Literature 15
    Information-Processing Constructivism Learning Theory 15
    Sociocultural Theory: Social Constructivism 17
    Multicultural Education 18
    Reading in the Content Area 21

Chapter 3: Methodology 28
    Participants 28
    Instrument 29
    Procedures 31
    Data Analysis and Reporting Plan 37

Chapter 4: Results 41
    Raw Score Data and Statistical Tests 41
    The Intervention's Impact: Comparing Study and Norming Groups 44

Chapter 5: Discussion 48
    Overview of the Applied Dissertation 48
    Implications of Findings 50
    Limitations of the Study 52
    Recommendations 53

References 55

Appendixes
    A BDA Chart 59
    B Concept Mapping 61
    C Structures Notes 62

Tables
    1 Statistically Significant Achievement Increases 43
    2 Educationally Meaningful Achievement Increases 44
    3 Evidence of Intervention's Effect on Achievement Gains 45

PREFACE

This book is the fruit of over fifty years of scholarship and of over forty-six years of teaching students in grades K–12 in general and special education classes and adults at the undergraduate and graduate levels.

The body of the book is the writer's unpublished dissertation: *Reading Instruction in a Content Area Course: Enhancing Secondary Students' Reading Achievement.*

This book is intended to be utilized by content-area teachers. Second, by education majors. Third, college education professors may want to guide their students through this book. Finally, principals may want to devote some in-service time to the study of this book. They may choose to invite interested teachers to use "before-during-after strategic reading process."

The Research Study

Donald Yokitis's research study took place in the fall term of the 2005–2006 school year in a high school in the northeast region of the United States. In addition to conducting the pretest, instruction, and posttest study, Donald Yokitis taught the psychology class in an eighty-minute block, five days a week.

The results of the research study were encouraging. Ten of the participating students realized statistically significant and educationally meaningful gains in reading comprehension. Nine participants scored the same on the standardize reading test from pretest to posttest. The scores of only three students decreased from pretest to posttest.

Caring

As was the case in Donald Yokitis's first book, *A Caring Errand: A Handbook for Educators, Future Educators, and Students' Caregivers*, care has the final say.

In the absence of caring, little good can occur in the lives of children and youth. When caring is present, many good things happen. Students make significant progress academically, socially, emotionally, vocationally, and psychologically. In addition, caring is the force that motivates the classroom practice of elementary, secondary, and special education teachers to empower students to strive for the moral maturity, which we hope is present in adults. In an increasingly diverse ethnic, racial, socioeconomic, religious, and educational world; embracing diversity is the only road to enable, not only schools, but all of the people to flourish in the here and now and in the future. Caring, without a doubt, makes the world of students and their involved adults go around.

ACKNOWLEDGMENTS

THE WRITER WISHES TO THANK a number of people who supported and encouraged him throughout the doctoral program. First, the students who participated in the research project are remembered with gratitude. Second, the writer appreciates the school's administrators for encouraging the study. Third, the technical support of Patty is greatly appreciated. Fourth, the writer is grateful for the expert guidance supplied by Dr. Ken Stothers, committee chair. Finally, a special thank-you is reserved for the writer's wife, Sue.

CHAPTER 1

Introduction

Statement of the Problem

THE SITE OF THE RESEARCH and intervention was an urban high school that serves approximately one thousand students. A degree of diversity exists in the high school. Of the student body, 74 percent are White, 24 percent are African American, and 2 percent are Hispanic or Asian.

Located in the northeast section of the United States, the small city where the school is situated is a community that has been in economic decline for some time. The metropolitan region is now one of the country's highest areas of unemployment. The unemployment rate of families with school-age children is 33 percent. Fifty percent of all residents under the age of eighteen live in poverty. Eighty-five percent of the high school's pupils qualify for free or reduced-priced lunch.

Although the area faces serious economic concerns, positive assets abound. The population is sustained by a strong work ethic and a family values heritage. Community and school leaders are committed to economic development. A central aspect of the focus is the positive role envisioned for the new high school. Two significant changes have occurred in the school district within the past three years that impacted the study. First, the district has adopted and implemented the Talent Development High School with Career Academies reform model (Johns Hopkins University 1994). Innovations included in the Ninth Grade Success Academy, component of the model that impacted the research and is discussed further. Second, a new high school was constructed. Students, staff, and community members are enjoying and taking pride in being a part of the $42 million school. No longer do students refer to the high school in derisive terms. Enthusiasm and hope have largely usurped feelings of listlessness and hopelessness in primacy.

Five wings structure the building. One section accommodates the ninth graders, and the other four house academies that provide curriculum and direction that prepare students for postsecondary education within broad career areas. In addition, a wide array of vocational-educational options is available to students. The school has been enlivened through a spirit of renewal that has the promise of elevating student achievement and the life of the broader community. It was the purpose of this writer's research and intervention project to contribute to the realization of these possibilities. This writer served in a collaborative effort to pilot a program of reading instruction in a content-area subject. The short-term objective was to empower participating students to realize significant increases in reading achievement. The long-term goal was to encourage strategic reading instruction in every course requiring reading at the school.

Since the 2003–2004 school year, approximately 50 percent of the incoming freshman class has tested two or more grade levels below ninth grade on the Gates-MacGinitie Reading Tests (MacGinitie, MacGinitie, Maria, and Dreyer 2000a). On the most recent state reading assessment, approximately 50 percent of the eleventh graders scored below proficiency. The school was under scrutiny by the state and needed to realize adequate yearly progress goals in reading, mathematics, and writing to avoid intervention. In addition, the high school was tasked with meeting reading and other curricula demands of the Middle States Association of College and Schools in order to retain accreditation.

Since the 2001–2002 school year, approximately 30 percent of the freshman class failed to earn a high school diploma at the conclusion of four years. A serious attendance problem persisted. The daily absentee rate averaged 10 percent. Through the implementation of the reform model, the comprehensive course offerings, and numerous policy and instructional initiatives, dedicated professionals addressed those concerns.

The writer's research was fashioned to contribute to the broader collaborative effort to enhance the performance of the school and the achievement of students. The study was designed to support the school's quests to strengthen the reading competencies of secondary students. A discrepancy existed between the preferred level of reading achievement and the actual level of performance. Approximately 50 percent of the school's students were reading below proficiency according to the Gates-MacGinitie Reading Tests (MacGinitie, et al. 2000a) and the state reading assessment.

In addition to placing the school's autonomy in jeopardy, the state of affairs put many students at a disadvantage in the competition for postsecondary educational placements and in realizing career goals. Families and the community were also burdened when young people entered the community lacking adequate preparation to serve their own needs and those of others productively and responsibly.

The National Assessment of Educational Progress (NAEP) 1998 Reading Report Card (as cited in Donahue, Voelkl, Campbell, and Mazzeo 1999) revealed that 66 percent of middle school and 73 percent of high school students were reading at or below basic level. Riley (1996) found that, for individuals with disabilities, the illiteracy rate could be as high as 73 percent. The concerns associated with limited reading competence have been documented in the research literature. Joel (1996) established that high school students reading significantly below grade-level expectation have lower self-esteem, exhibit greater discipline issues, and are more likely to drop out of school than are competent readers. The United States Department of Labor (1998) *Work Force Report* disclosed that adults with reading deficiencies are more likely, than able readers, to be unemployed and impoverished.

Research has established that students who fail to achieve basic reading skills by the conclusion of third grade will probably face reading challenges throughout their school careers and into adulthood (Bryant 2003). Donahue et al. disclosed that, at the eighth-grade level, 32 percent of boys and

19 percent of girls were below basic level. In the twelfth grade, 30 percent of boys and 17 percent of girls failed to perform at the basic level. Bryant pointed out that the performance gap between inefficient and efficient readers may continue to widen as the demands made by content-area curriculum on reading capabilities increase.

In addition, the 1997 reauthorization of the Individuals with Disabilities Act in identifying the regular education setting as the appropriate placement for all students created the necessity for meeting the needs of increasing numbers of troubled readers in regular classrooms. Struggling secondary students require effective interventions to enable them to acquire reading strategies and self-regulating practices necessary to successfully comprehend content-area texts.

The underlying problem, that was the focus of the writer's study, was that the school's educators were inadequately informed. The overall reading achievement of the school's students was unacceptably low. At the same time, whereas effective reading techniques were available to enhance the reading competencies of high school students, those tactics were rarely utilized in the general education courses in which the majority of the high school's struggling readers were being schooled.

The writer was centrally involved in the research study intended to address the reading concern at the high school and to contribute to the literature on strategic reading instruction in high school content-area classes. The writer was responsible for implementation of the project's one-group, pretest-posttest design during the 2005–2006 school year. The intervention entailed the integration of strategic reading instruction into a psychology course. The writer was the psychology teacher who provided direction and instruction in reading strategies and guided daily practice of the tactics. In addition, the writer was responsible for securing the school district's approval for the study. The school's superintendent granted permission to the investigator to conduct the study.

Purpose of the Project

The high school community, under consideration, began to address the reading concern that has been identified at the ninth-grade level and persisted through the eleventh grade, according to available data. Freshmen reading two or more years below grade expectation were assigned to the Strategic Reading course. In addition, the Freshman Seminar course provided direct instruction in reading and study skills. While the Gates-MacGinitie Reading Tests (MacGinitie et al. 2000a) were administered to eighth-grade students and served as a pretest, no posttests were administered. School officials, therefore, did not have data available to judge the effectiveness of the Strategic Reading and Freshman Seminar courses.

The writer's study was designed to support and extend current efforts by introducing specific reading strategy instruction and practice into a content-area classroom. Although students are taught a number of comprehension tactics in the Ninth Grade Academy programming, the strategies have not been intentionally applied in content classes. The writer's project represented the first concerted effort to directly instruct students in reading strategies and require consistent practice of the tactics in a regular education course.

The purpose of the research project was to determine the impact of reading strategies instruction on reading achievement in a psychology class. It was the more encompassing goal of the study to encourage reading instruction in every course that required reading at the secondary school. Finally, the research was intended to contribute to the literature on high school reading instruction.

Research Question

A single research question was fashioned to achieve the study's purpose. The question that directed the research project was: will students receiving reading-strategies instruction in a content-area class realize statistically significant and educationally meaningful gains in reading comprehension achievement?

Definition of Terms

A number of specific terms are used throughout this applied dissertation. For the purpose of this applied dissertation, the following terms are defined:

Dependent variable. For the purpose of this applied dissertation, this term refers to the reading level of the participating students.
Independent variable. For the purpose of this study, this term refers to the strategic reading treatment.
Information-processing constructivism theory. This phrase refers to a learning theory that perceives the learner as actively processing information and constructing new knowledge.
Metacognition. This term refers to the awareness of thinking.
Multicultural education. This phrase refers to a reform movement that intends to change schools so that students from diverse racial, cultural, social class, and disability classification will secure educational equality.
Sociocultural theory. This phrase refers to a learning theory that views all learning as socially mediated, with the learner actively constructing knowledge through interactions with others.

CHAPTER 2

Review of the Related Literature

Two learning theories underpin the pedagogical approach selected in this research project that intended to furnish the instruction necessary for students to achieve significant growth in reading capacity: (a) information-processing constructivism (Mayer 1996) and (b) sociocultural theory (Berk 2002). The literature review begins with a focus on the first learning theory. Attention is then directed to the sociocultural perspective. Next, the multicultural education approach that provides for the process and context required for instruction in strategic reading is presented in association with sociocultural theory. The discussion then focuses on a theory of student empowerment. Thereafter, current conceptions of the reading process are presented and linked to the learning theories and pedagogical approach. Finally, the reading strategies that have theoretical and empirical support are put forth and examined. The discussion relates the specific strategies to the research study's theoretical and pedagogical bases and to the study's methodology.

Information-Processing Constructivism Learning Theory

The study is underpinned by two variations of the general theory of constructivism: (a) information-processing constructivism and (b) social constructivism or specifically, sociocultural theory. In the 1960s, information-processing theory arose as the dominant learning theory and remained the controlling model through the 1970s. Berk (2002) advanced a standard definition: "Information processing [is] an approach that views the human mind as a symbol-manipulating system through which information flows and regards cognitive development as continuous" (p. 23). The theory proceeded on the foundation of a human-computer analogy.

The digital computer, for information-processing theorists, serves as a metaphor for human learning. Cognitive psychologists observed that both the computer and the human mind engaged in cognitive processes such as acquiring knowledge, remembering, making decisions, and solving problems. The electronic digital computer is viewed as performing cognitive tasks in processing information. Symbols are taken in as input, operations are applied to the input, and output is provided. Information-processing theorists perceive human learning similarly. Humans are regarded as information processors. Learning is the process of acquiring knowledge (Mayer 1996).

The thought processes, or thinking skills, applied in processing information are less fully propagated in children than in adults. Education is, in part, an effort to foster the full maturation of cognitive skills. Berk (2002) maintained, "Mental strategies are the procedures that operate on and transform information, thereby increasing the efficiency and flexibility of thinking and the chances that information will be retained" (p. 224).

Information-processing theorists have found that the amount of information and speed at which information can be effectively handled increase with age and make possible more complex thinking (Case 1998). Although brain growth partially accounts for the greater information processing capabilities, problem-solving and comprehension strategies expand and are further cultivated with development. In addition, a vast knowledge base contributes to the increased capabilities noted.

A final aspect of information-processing theory bears significantly on the application of the theory to education. Metacognition, or awareness of thinking, expands during adolescence and leads to insights into effective tactics for acquiring information and for solving problems. Cognitive self-regulation is critical in the learning process. Self-regulation refers to monitoring and adjusting one's thinking.

Information-processing theory contributes significantly to the understanding of the learning process. Current conceptions of learning include information-processing constructs. The thought processes or mental strategies of perception, attention, memory, classification, planning, problem-solving, evaluation, application, and comprehension are generally accepted by learning theorists as essential in the process of constructing knowledge. Metacognitive habits and self-regulation skills are recognized as crucial to the individual's endeavor to build knowledge through employing cognitive strategies (Berk 2002).

The learner in the information-processing model is regarded as an active, sense-making being. However, the educational application of the model has resulted in promoting conditions that have placed the learner in a somewhat passive position. The learner's perceived role as receiver of knowledge and the teacher's assumed role as dispenser of knowledge have led to the prevailing teacher-centered instructional model. In schooling, the theory tends to promote a model of an active teacher dispensing information and a less active student receiving information. The positive contributions to educational practice made by information-processing theory are of great magnitude. The focus on cognitive or learning strategies and on self-regulated learning provides the theoretical underpinnings for the worthy educational goal of fostering the growth of students as independent and empowered learners. Nevertheless, the promise of information-processing theory to supply a firm foundation for educational practice awaited a merger with constructivist theory (Mayer 1996).

In the 1980s, cognitive psychologists increasingly expanded research beyond laboratories. As research moved into the world, advances were made in the psychologies of reading, writing, mathematics, and science learning. The goal was to learn how people learn to read, write, and think mathematically and scientifically. The result was a constructivist revolution with cognitive psychology becoming a science vitally relevant educationally (Mayer 1996). Today, educational and cognitive psychologists believe that learning is a form of active knowledge construction (Derry 1996).

The constructivist approach to understanding learning focuses on the learner as actively building knowledge. Cognitive constructivism is perceived today as a metaphorical assumption about the structure and functioning of cognition. Derry (1996) maintained that most cognitive researchers accept the constructivist's basic assumption that learning is knowledge construction. Derry further established that constructivism has embraced the modern information-processing conception of learning. The resulting information-processing constructivism theory is one in which information has been reinterpreted as knowledge and processing reformulated as constructing. Learning is conceived of in terms of a learner actively selecting, organizing, and integrating incoming experiences with existing knowledge. The learner constructs new knowledge through a process of (a) selecting relevant incoming experiences, (b) employing cognitive strategies to organize the experiences into coherent patterns, and (c) integrating the organized patterns into existing knowledge (Mayer 1996).

Information-processing constructivism overcomes two limitations of classical information-processing theory: (a) the tendency to view the learner as a somewhat passive receiver of information and (b) the failure to take into account the affective, social, and cultural aspects of cognition and learning (Mayer 1996). A more thorough response to the need to take into account the affective, social and cultural elements in learning is found in the concepts and educational implications of a genre of sociocultural constructivism that is sociocultural theory.

Sociocultural Theory: Social Constructivism

The second theoretical foundation for the investigation and intervention is the sociocultural learning theory. This systematic formulation supports and frames much of the contemporary instructional effort to enable students to grow cognitively and to construct knowledge. In this part of the literature review, sociocultural theory is examined. During the course of the analysis, the presentation transitions into an examination of multicultural education that shapes the pedagogical approach employed in this dissertation's study.

Sociocultural theory, which has evolved from the work of Russian psychologist Lev Vygotsky (1896–1934), maintains that children and youth attain a culture's ways of thinking and behaving through cooperative dialogue with adults and more knowledgeable peers. These social interactions are essential for the transmission of the values, beliefs, customs, and skills of a culture to younger members (Berk 2002). The communication between the more knowledgeable and less knowledgeable group members becomes part of the learner's thinking.

A number of instructional concepts and practices have emerged from this theory of learning: (a) intersubjectivity, (b) assisted discovery, (c) peer collaboration, (d) scaffolding (Berk 2002), and (e) cultural relevance (Banks and McGee Banks 2004). Newson and Newson (1975) defined intersubjectivity as the process by which two participants who begin a task with divergent conceptions arrive at a common understanding. For example, although a student and a teacher may initially have different ideas about what it means to establish a reading purpose, they eventually arrive at a shared conception. The teacher's attention and support foster the student's achievement of the understanding. For instance, the instructor may employ assisted discovery in guiding the learner to attain an accurate conception of setting a purpose for reading. Explanations, demonstrations, and verbal prompts are utilized to direct the learning process in assisted discovery (Berk).

Peer collaboration involves employing cooperative learning groups to guide students through the process of achieving new knowledge and skills (Alfassi 2004, Berk 2002). For example, students varying in abilities and levels of conceptual understanding may assist one another in the practice of formulating reading goals. Scaffolding supports the ultimate goal of constructing knowledge and independently employing learning strategies. The quality of social support is changed over the course of the instructional session (Berk). Continuing the example, the beginning stage of direct instruction in and modeling of setting a reading purpose transitions into guided discovery. Less intrusive support is then provided through peer collaboration. Finally, additional guidance may be required as students independently practice establishing reading purposes. Throughout learning sessions, the utilization of culturally relevant reading materials is recommended. Banks and McGee Banks (2004) advised teachers to employ reading texts that contain information familiar to culturally diverse students. The use of texts containing varied elements of popular adolescent culture has been promoted by a number of theorists and researchers (Banks and McGee Banks, Stevens 2001).

The writer reviewed the pedagogical approach that provides for the application of theory in practice. The instructional process central in empowering learners to acquire reading strategies includes the practices of multicultural education. This pedagogical approach seeks to provide well for the instructional programming of schools with diverse populations of students. The multicultural education approach answers the need of this dissertation's project to apply an appropriate method of instruction to a diverse population of learners.

Multicultural Education

The multicultural education approach to the structuring and functioning of schools emerged from the foundation of sociocultural learning theory and in response to changing demographics and a heightened awareness of America's failure to achieve educational equality and overall excellence (Banks and McGee Banks 2004). Troy (1999) noted that (a) two million pupils do not speak English and (b) six million youngsters are limited in the use of English. In 2000, 40 percent of students in Grades one to twelve were students of color (Banks and McGee Banks).

Neither widespread academic excellence nor educational equality has been realized in America. Achievement in the most fundamental academic skill, reading, is of particular concern. The NAEP 1998 Reading Report Card (as cited in Donahue et al. 1999) established that 66 percent of middle school and 73 percent of high school students are reading at or below basic level. Students of nonmainstream cultures are disproportionately placed in special education programs (Kea and Utley 1998). Bryant (2003) noted that pupils of African American, American Indian, and Hispanic backgrounds and youngsters living in poverty achieve at lower levels compared to their middle-class European American peers. The reading attainment of students with disabilities and pupils of nondominant cultures is significantly lower than that of middle-class White students (Schmidt, Rozendal, and Greenman 2002).

Multicultural education is a reform movement intended to change the schooling process so that students from all social-class, racial, language, cultural, and disability groups have an equal opportunity to excel (Banks, and McGee Banks 2004). The reform movement began in the 1990s. Multicultural education is an ethical commitment that acknowledges and values culturally diverse individuals (Day-Vines 2000). Turnbull and Turnbull (2001) advanced a broad conception of culture to encompass race, ethnicity, religion, geographic location, socioeconomic class, sexual orientation, gender, and disability status.

Connecting school and home cultures. Much of the multicultural education literature is dominated by discussions concerning the nature, consequences, and remediation of discontinuities that exist between the home cultures of minority group students and Eurocentric school cultures (Banks and McGee Banks 2004). The instructional practices, behavioral expectations, and curriculum content of many schools fit well with the home cultures of middle-class European American students. Conversely, students of color often need to cope with instructional methods, behavioral requirements, and learning materials that are not culturally relevant. Multicultural theorists view the achievement gap between European American students and pupils of nondominant cultural backgrounds as, in part, a result of cultural mismatch (Matczynski, Rogus, Lasley, and Joseph 2000).

The multicultural education approach, on the foundation of a sociocultural learning theory, seeks to utilize the cultural backgrounds and experiences of culturally diverse students (Matczynski et al., 2000). Congruency between home and classroom cultures is advanced when curriculum is related to the learner's familiar world outside of school and when instructional processes take into account the unique learning styles of culturally diverse students (Matczynski et al., Reglin 1995).

Two aspects of multicultural education are centrally important to the instructional approach employed in the reading intervention that intends to empower readers. The actual process of teaching the reading strategies that empower readers, by its very nature, creates (a) consistent connections between school and home cultures of students and (b) a warm, collaborative classroom environment. Whereas the former aspect of multicultural education has already been detailed, the latter element is the subject of the next section.

Classroom environment. Multicultural education embedded in ethical practice requires that learning environment and student-teacher relationships are shaped to support the growth of all students in diverse classrooms. Sociocultural theory, the epistemological substructure for multicultural education, determined that knowledge and skills are primarily, socially, and culturally constructed (Berk 2002). The classroom context of the learning process is important in the educational approach and learning theory under consideration. The classroom teacher is called on to establish the welcoming climate and the warm interpersonal relationships that foster learning (Collinson 1999).

The welcoming and supportive classroom climate develops on the foundation of warm student-teacher rapport and when trust, honesty, discipline, respect, and care are present at all times (Reglin 1995). The overarching goal of student learning focuses all interactions and processes (Collinson 1999). The classroom is nurturing and warm (Reglin). Each student is equally welcome. Community is built through the consistent practices of tolerance and understanding of differences and the acknowledgement of the common aspirations, values, and needs that bind individuals together (Turnbull and Turnbull 2001).

It is the underlying assumption of this dissertation's writer that the interactive and collaborative manner in which reading strategies are necessarily taught and learned tends to create a classroom environment that provides the social support for the development of empowered readers. The next section presents the nature of student empowerment through a discussion of a theory of empowerment based on the fostering of students' motivation and knowledge/skill resources. The ensuing presentation lays the groundwork for the discussion of reading in the content area where the learning process tends to strengthen learners to grow as self-motivated and self-monitoring readers.

Student empowerment. A widely accepted educational goal is to enhance the growth of students as self-motivated and self-regulated learners (Berk 2002). Turnbull and Turnbull (2001) provided a framework that serves to conceptualize and organize efforts toward achieving the goal. The theorists advanced an approach to strengthening people based on collaboration.

Empowerment entails gaining control over one's life and actively pursuing one's needs and wants. Empowerment occurs within a social context. In the case of students, the context involves the classroom environment and the interactions and the relationships among the pupils and between the students and the teacher. Turnbull and Turnbull (2001) found that collaborative climate and relationships promote the strengthening of students. Student empowerment is enhanced through the strengthening and activating of motivational knowledge/skill resources.

Turnbull and Turnbull (2001) identified five components of the motivational resource: (a) self-efficacy, (b) personal-control, (c) high expectations, (d) energy, and (e) persistence. Self-efficacy lies at the core of motivation. A belief in one's personal abilities is central to a willingness to engage in an activity. Students' behaviors are significantly influenced by their feelings of self-efficacy. Students tend to avoid activities when they sense they cannot succeed and to participate when they feel competent. For example, capable readers choose to engage actively with texts, whereas struggling readers often avoid reading or find it difficult to commit fully to the task. Through proper support and instruction, the reluctant reader's knowledge base and strategic reading skills can be bolstered. As knowledge and skills increase so does self-efficacy.

Personal control, the second aspect of motivational resources, entails a belief in the individual's ability to effectively impact what happens to him or her (Turnbull and Turbull 2001). In a collaborative classroom climate, many decisions are reached cooperatively; some are made by the individual student. Such an arrangement tends to foster a sense of personal control in students.

The third component of motivational resources is high expectations. Collaborative processes and relationships foster motivation. In a cooperative classroom atmosphere, while the teacher encourages students to set high goals, the responsibility for achieving the visions is shared. A shared vision tends to encourage effort (Reglin 1995).

The final two elements of motivational resources posited by Turnbull and Turnbull (2001) were considered together. Energy and persistence entail the gathering and sustaining of physical, mental, and emotional assets in order to undertake activities and pursue them to completion. Reglin (1995) determined that students are disposed to commit to academic tasks and persist in their efforts when warm rapport exists with their instructors and cooperative environment prevails.

The vision that propelled the research and intervention was the strengthening of readers through the mastery of reading strategies. The literature, so far reviewed, laid much of the theoretical and pedagogical foundations for the study's methodology. Before a detailed description of the research study's methodology can be presented, the literature review needs to focus on reading in the content area and specific reading strategies, as well as a discussion of how reading strategies may be effectively applied in content-area courses to enhance the reader's skills.

Reading in the Content Area

Reading is an active cognitive process. It is an exercise that takes place in the mind. Through the mental acrobatics occurring during the interaction between a reader and text, the learner is able to construct meaning (Johns and Lenski 2001). Cognitive strategies are applied to a text throughout the activity, in which existing knowledge and new knowledge are integrated to create meaning (Alexander and Jetton 2000). The skill and knowledge resources of the reader are mutually supportive. Strategic reading skills enable the learner to comprehend effectively or build knowledge from texts. The accumulative reservoir of information allows the reader to construct new knowledge more efficiently by connecting new information with a large knowledge base (Berk 2002).

Reading is the cognitive activity in which information is processed and knowledge is built in a sustained interaction between a reader and text. The interaction is sustained through self-regulation, which Berk (2002) described as "the continuously monitoring process toward a goal, checking outcomes and redirecting unsuccessful efforts" (p. 449). Self-regulated or active and focused reading is achieved when learners utilize reading strategies during engagements with texts. From the information processing constructivism perspective, the key to enhancing the reading achievement of students is the empowerment realized through the mastery of reading strategies.

Although reading is a cognitive activity, it is, as with all learning, socially mediated. The cognitive processes necessary to construct knowledge from text develop through interactions with others, including more knowledgeable adults and peers (Berk 2002). Whereas the individual reader alone must perform the required cognitive tasks and employ effective self-regulation in order to read successfully, the social context critically impacts the reader's success or failure. According to Vacca and Vacca (2002), in the classroom setting where the learning process intends to strengthen readers, "Learning is as much collaborative as it is individual" (p. 23).

Motivation underpins all learning. Self-motivation is required of students to sustain efforts when mastering the reading tactics that are the means by which self-regulated reading is achieved. Research on motivation to learn has established that meeting individual learners' needs for control, competence, and belonging is essential in fostering self-motivation (McCombs and Barton 1998). The content-area teacher, by assuming the dispositions and practices of the multicultural teacher, fosters self-motivation in students. The reader's need for control, competence, and belonging is addressed by the teacher's effective application of multicultural pedagogy to classroom relationships and to the learning process.

To begin with, an alliance between teacher and learner is forged when they embrace a common vision of student success and when the responsibility for achieving the goal is shared. Feeling connected with others heightens energy and persistence and feelings of positive expectations and self-efficacy (Turnbull and Turnbull 2001). The adolescent who struggles in reading finds the energy to persist in reading tasks when supported by a strong collaborative relationship with the teacher and others.

Second, multicultural literature and motivational research findings established the importance of connecting students' interests and experiences with the school's curriculum. The secondary classroom teacher has the option of supplementing required texts with reading materials of multicultural and popular culture genre. Focused reading that results in constructing knowledge and refining reading skills most readily occurs when students are naturally motivated by texts that interest them and connect with their experiences (Bean 2000).

The teacher can additionally strengthen the reader's motivation and knowledge/skill resources by structuring lessons requiring reading. The lesson design is based on a conception of reading as a strategic process comprised of before (B), during (D), and after (A) reading stages (see Appendix A). The BDA formulation is widely supported in the literature (Alfassi 2004, Johns and Lenski 2001, Shaw, Roe, and Legters 2000; Vacca and Vacca 2002). The goal of reading is to construct meaning effectively from texts. In order to succeed consistently, the learner must be motivated and self-regulated throughout the reading process. The reader's motivation and knowledge/skill resources need to be actively engaged. The manner of structuring lessons demanding reading bears significantly on the degree of student engagement or disengagement.

An alternative to the traditional method of assigning a text and answering questions procedure entails the structuring of lessons explicitly to require the application of reading strategies to the text throughout the prereading, reading, and post-reading stages of the reading process. The reader's needs for control and competence are met when the instructional approach shifts the primary responsibility for learning in content-area classes to the student. When the student is empowered by the acquisition of effective reading strategies, he or she gains competence and control over learning. The reader is able to construct knowledge effectively from texts. Throughout the reading process, thoughtful instruction encourages the reader's focused engagement with the text (Shaw et al. 2000).

The final section of the literature review presents a number of specific research-based reading strategies that fit within the BDA reading framework. The conclusion of this chapter focuses the review of the literature on the research study.

Reading strategies. Shaw et al. (2000) provided, in outline form, the essentials of the first specific reading strategy under consideration, the SQ3R study strategy. The *S* asks a student to survey the text before reading. Items identifying the structure of the selection, including headings and illustrations, are previewed. Students, next, formulate questions (the *Q*) that they believe could be answered by reading the text. The three *R*s represent read, recite, and review. Students are to read carefully. In reciting, students are called on to reflect on what they have read and to answer the questions they have constructed. In reviewing, readers are encouraged to conduct a review after reading and to take notes on the most important information found in the selection.

SQ3R requires students to use textbook features, identify main ideas and supporting details, construct questions, summarize, and take notes. Johns and Lenski (2001), therefore, emphasized the importance of directly instructing students in the use of this reading strategy and of modeling the process. The ultimate goal is for students to master the process.

Although little research regarding the effectiveness of SQ3R has been conducted, it remained an option to consider on the basis of answering the demands of current learning and reading theories. SQ3R promotes active and self-regulated reading and construction of knowledge from texts (Quiocho 1997). This strategy, which really is a package of study techniques, is theoretically sound. SQ3R answers the requirements of information-processing constructivism theory by elevating the metacognitive awareness of students as they survey or preview the reading selection. The cognitive demands of the text are anticipated through the process of surveying. Purposeful and self-regulated reading is stimulated when students read to answer the questions they formulated. Knowledge is effectively constructed when students share the answers to their questions and take notes that summarize significant facts and concepts (Johns and Lenski 2001).

SQ3R, when supported through instruction and modeling and collaboratively practiced as a class or in small groups, satisfies the demands of sociocultural learning theory and multicultural education practice. Students learn from their teacher and from one another. Scaffolding is essential to enabling students to master the multifaceted technique that is learned in cooperative learning groups or interactively as a class.

The second reading tactic much discussed in the secondary reading instruction literature had research support for its effectiveness. Reciprocal teaching promotes four strategic behaviors employed to comprehension of texts. Questioning, clarifying, summarizing, and predicting are the tactics taught and practiced in this instructional approach. The goal of reciprocal teaching is for each student to eventually apply the process independently. After direct instruction and modeling, the teacher gradually hands over responsibilities to students (Slater and Horstman 2002). Alfassi (2004) explicitly combined direct explanation with reciprocal teaching. Fisher (2001) pointed out that this strategy contributed to the increased reading achievement realized by one high school committed to elevating the literacy climate of the school and the reading performance of students.

Reciprocal teaching, which conforms to the requirements of the information-processing constructivism model of learning, and with current understandings of reading, was summarized by Slater and Horstman (2002) in four steps that follow the reading of a short text:

1. Questions are posed. The leader or a group member formulates questions generated by the reading and members of the group answer them.
2. Issues are clarified. The leader or group members resolve problems.
3. The selection is summarized. The leader or a group member presents a summary.
4. Predictions are made. The leader or group members make predictions about upcoming selections.

Alfassi (2004) detailed the workings of reciprocal teaching in a study that coupled the strategy with direct instruction in its use. Reciprocal reading is a tactic that fosters reading as a group problem-solving activity. Active and self-regulated reading is promoted by a process that stimulates readers to think while reading (Palinscar and Brown 1984). The four steps of the comprehension strategy are applied as students read the selection paragraph by paragraph. Scaffolding advances students toward the ultimate goal of competence in employing the strategy independently.

The objective of Alfassi's (2004) study was to investigate the effectiveness of reading strategy instruction in a ninth-grade English class. A pretest-posttest-comparison-group design was employed. Alfassi's hypothesis was that the treatment group would show greater improvement than the comparison group in reading comprehension. Data were collected concerning two dependent variables. The students were given reading assessments and a standardized reading comprehension test before and after the intervention. The reading assessments were similar to teacher-constructed quizzes. The standardized test was the Gates-MacGinitie Reading Comprehension Test (MacGinitie et al. 2000a). The results supported the hypothesis on both measures. The results of the study demonstrated the educational benefits of incorporating the reciprocal teaching strategy with direct instruction into a secondary-level English class.

Reciprocal teaching is a reading strategy that is theoretically sound. The requirements of the information-processing constructivism model and those of sociocultural learning theory are met by the multifaceted reading strategy. Metacognitive awareness and self-regulated reading are enhanced through active reading structured throughout the processes of questioning, summarizing, clarifying, and predicting. Scaffolding enables students to benefit from the knowledge and skills of their teacher while the collaborative and interactive learning process capitalizes on the social interactions among peers that promote learning.

The third specific reading strategy under examination here is KWL. Students are engaged in focused text learning in a three-step process. The strategy begins by having students recall what they know (K) about the topic. Second, students are asked to establish a purpose for reading by positing questions in terms of what they want (W) to learn about the topic. Third, what was learned (L) is summarized (Vacca and Vacca 2002).

KWL needs to be thoroughly taught, modeled, and practiced. Ogle (1986) maintained that it is important for the teacher to address the motivation needs of students throughout the process of guiding students to mastery of the KWL strategy. As the teacher explains and models the strategy, students may come to understand how their need to connect with text, and others, and to control learning by reading can be fulfilled (Vacca and Vacca 2002).

The initial instruction and modeling of the KWL strategy occurs with a group of learners or with the entire class. Vacca and Vacca (2002) summarized the instructional process in six steps:

1. The KWL strategy is introduced in conjunction with a text selection. The teacher introduces the strategy.
2. Students are guided to identify what they think they know about the topic. After the teacher introduces the topic of the reading selection, the class engages in brainstorming. The teacher writes their ideas on the board.
3. Students are led to generate questions. The group or class is asked to consider what they want to know more about regarding the topic. The teacher records all the questions on the board. After all the questions have been written on the board, students are asked to record the questions they personally want to have answered by reading.
4. Students are guided to anticipate the organization of the text selection. As part of the prereading stage, students are encouraged to use their prior knowledge of the topic and

their questions to make predictions about the selection's organization. The teacher records predictions on the board. Students make individual choices and record these.
5. Students read the text to answer questions. While actively reading, students record answers to their questions and make notes for new ideas and information. A discussion follows the reading focused on sharing answers.
6. Students are steered into follow-up activities. Post-reading activities serve to clarify and expand learning.

Research has largely supported the efficacy of this approach to reading that entails the eliciting of prior knowledge, formulating a reading purpose, and summarizing learning (Fisher 2001). The refinement of the cognitive skills of attending, elaborating, and problem-solving is implicit in KWL. New learning is constructed with reference to previously learned material. The KWL strategy is a theoretically sound means of answering the requirements of the information-processing model of learning and of current reading theory. Additionally, the tactic is consistent with sociocultural theory and multicultural education practice. Through the interactive and cooperative process of learning, students learn from their teacher and from one another.

The fourth reading strategy that is prominent in the literature and supported by research is vocabulary instruction (Bryant, Ugel, Thompson, and Hamff 1999; Fisher 2001, Vacca and Vacca 2002). A strong connection exists between vocabulary knowledge and reading comprehension. In content-area courses, knowledge of subject-specific and technical vocabulary is essential to construct knowledge from texts effectively (Vacca and Vacca). Fisher stressed the contribution made by vocabulary instruction in the reading performance of high school students in a comprehensive initiative that included vocabulary instruction among a number of specific reading strategies.

The learner's venture to construct content-area knowledge can be supported. Vacca and Vacca (2002) suggested, "Teachers can help students build conceptual knowledge of content area terms by teaching and reinforcing the concept words in relation to other concept words" (p. 165). Teachers can enhance the student's endeavor to create conceptual networks by providing the guidance necessary for students to achieve an understanding of key terms.

Vocabulary instruction may occur before, during, and after reading. Prior to reading specialized vocabulary can be introduced and related to the students' background experiences and knowledge. While reading, readers can focus attention on important terms by recording them in notes. After reading, learners can extend and deepen understandings of the topic and vocabulary through post-reading activities (Vacca and Vacca 2002).

A vocabulary instruction strategy that supports students in constructing conceptual knowledge is semantic/concept mapping. This strategy is consistently recommended in the literature on reading instruction (Bryant et al. 1999, Fisher 2001, Johns and Lenski 2001, Shaw et al. 2000). Semantic maps are a type of graphic organizer that involves a process that helps students to connect prior knowledge with new vocabulary and to see the relationships among concepts (see Appendix B). Bryant et al. proposed the following steps to construct concept maps as a class or in small groups: (a) identify the topic and place it in the middle of the graphic organizer, (b) brainstorm words that are associated with the subject matter, (c) discuss the meanings of the words and how to group them into categories, (d) create labels for the classes, (e) produce words or subcategories for each category, and (f) discuss the terms and the relationships among the categories and subcategories.

When students are engaged in actively studying vocabulary, the requirements of information-processing and sociocultural learning theories, as well as the demands of multicultural educational practice, are answered. Students process information and construct conceptual knowledge more efficiently when afforded opportunities to connect new vocabulary and background knowledge. The collaborative process of scaffolding through instruction and modeling and in creating graphic organizers provides for the social support of cognitive learning. The warm and cooperative relationships and climate that characterize multicultural education are built as the teacher and students actively participate in the learning process.

Structured note-taking, the fifth reading strategy, is a system for taking notes that centers on identifying and retaining main ideas and supporting details (Smith and Tompkins 1988). Content-area texts are arranged according to structures fashioned by the authors (see Appendix C). Subject headings identify topics and subtopics in many textbooks. Graphs, pictures, and illustrations are other organizational components commonly found in content-area texts. A reader's skill in recognizing these structures enhances comprehension and retention of information and construction of knowledge (Fisher 2001).

Structured note-taking entails following the organization of the text in making notes within the framework of the classic outline. The note making technique may be employed during the initial reading of the selection or after reading as a study strategy to prepare students for quizzes or tests.

Vacca and Vacca (2002) advanced a procedure for scaffolding the learning of note making. Five steps are required:

1. The teacher assigns a text. Students make whatever notes they choose.
2. The class shares and discusses the notes. The difficulties entailed in note making are pinpointed.
3. The teacher provides students with a copy of a reading selection. While modeling taking notes, the instructor employs the think-aloud procedure to explain the reasoning that supports the note making choices.
4. Students practice note making in small groups. Peer-groups provide additional guidance to individual students.
5. Products generated by the cooperative groups are put on the board. The class evaluates the structured notes.
6. The teacher provides scaffolding as necessary. Individuals in groups or working independently are guided to strategy mastery.

Consistent with learning-processing constructivism learning theory, structured note-taking supports the reader in perceiving, attending, remembering, problem-solving, and constructing knowledge. Metacognitive habits and self-regulated learning are enhanced through the requirement to actively interact with the reading material.

In line with sociocultural theory and multicultural education practice, structured note-taking necessitates instruction and modeling by the teacher in entire class or small group collaborative learning. Sharing the responsibility for achievement and cooperatively interacting fosters warm relationships and a welcoming classroom environment.

Focusing the review on the study. The specific reading strategies previously reviewed lie at the heart of this applied dissertation. The methodology of the research project utilized the strategies in a manner that created the conditions that empowered students to read more effectively. The methodology focused on student mastery of a reading process involving a number of specific reading strategies. Through the methodology, the social and motivational supports necessary for the effective mastery of reading strategies and learning from texts were constructed. The learning process was the means by which student motivation, skill, and knowledge were enhanced and social support achieved.

CHAPTER 3

Methodology

THE PROBLEM AND RESEARCH QUESTION that directed the study were addressed through the implementation of the project's methodology. Approximately 50 percent of the incoming freshman class over the past several years has tested two to three grade levels below grade nine on the Gates-MacGinitie Reading Tests (MacGinitie et al., 2000a). On the latest state reading assessment, about 50 percent of the eleventh-grade class scored below proficiency. The writer intended to determine the effect on measured reading comprehension of incorporating strategic reading instruction into a psychology class. The data generated through the research served to answer the research question. Will students receiving reading strategies instruction in a content-area class realize statistically significant and educationally meaningful gains in reading comprehension achievement?

The potential benefit of the proposed study in contributing to the amelioration of the reading concern required an analysis of results. If educationally and statistically significant results were documented through the implementation of the strategic reading process designed for the project, content-area teachers in the school might be encouraged to utilize the reading tactics in their courses.

Participants

The students who participated in the study were eleventh and twelfth graders enrolled in a first-semester psychology class. The students elected to take the course and were registered through the school's standard scheduling process. The heterogeneous group represented the student body's ethnic, racial, academic, and socioeconomic diversity. Ten boys and twelve girls were in the study group. The racial cultural composition of the class was six students of African American heritage and sixteen of White American background. The academic levels included one student with a significant reading concern, seventeen students enrolled in various academic and vocational options afforded by the general education programming, and four students participating in the gifted curriculum. The socioeconomic composition of the group ranged from students eligible for reduce-price meals to those from upper middle-class families.

The writer was directly engaged throughout the entire research project. The writer administered the pre- and posttests, supplied direct instruction in and modeling of the strategic reading process, and guided practice of the specific reading tactics and process. In discharging the duty of the psychology instructor, the writer ensured that the strategic reading process was a central means by which the course content was mastered. The writer was responsible for scoring the tests and interpreting the assessment data.

Instrument

The Fourth Edition Gates-MacGinite Reading Comprehension Test (GMRCT; MacGinitie et al. 2000a) is widely cited in the literature on strategic and secondary reading as a means of assessing levels of reading achievement (Alfassi 2004). The measure consists of eleven passages of a variety of prose. Each selection is followed by several multiple-choice questions. The test is designed to measure a student's ability to construct meaning from texts. The forty-eight questions of the Level 10/12 GMRCT require the construction of meaning based on information that is explicitly stated in the selection and on information that is only implicit in the selections. Both literal and inferential comprehension capabilities of students are assessed by the test (MacGinitie, MacGinitie, Maria, and Dreyer 2002).

The authors of the GMRCT Level 10/12 and a team of teachers selected the eleven passages from a diverse pool of sources. The test development process was designed to supply a set of passages, and comprehension questions that are representative of the materials students are required to read and of the kinds of questions students are asked to answer in school (MacGinitie et al. 2002).

Significant information supporting both the validity and reliability of the GMRCT are advanced by MacGinitie et al. (2002). The claim of the test developers that the GMRCT can help determine how well groups of students are reading and how well they are progressing is of central importance to the writer's study and supported by theoretical argumentation and data concerning the validity, reliability, and standardization process of the measure.

The Gates-MacGinitie Reading Tests were standardized, following a stratified random sample design. Almost sixty-five thousand students from all parts of the United States provided a culturally and socioeconomic diverse sample. The test developers established that the representative sample utilized in their standardization is the foundation for the validity of inferences concerning individual and group scores on the norm-referenced test (MacGinitie et al. 2002).

In addition to supplying substantial evidence that the GMRCT was properly standardized, to be used with culturally and socioeconomic diverse groups of students, MacGinitie et al. (2002) reported appropriate comprehension test reliability and alternate form reliabilities. The validity of the scores on the alternate forms of the GMRCT utilized as this dissertation study's pretest and posttest rested on the overall reliability of the test and on the alternate forms reliability. GMRCT Level 10/12 alternate form reliability for students in grade eleven and for those in grade twelve is a mean of .82. The reliability coefficient significantly exceeds the minimum recommended coefficient for reporting group scores of .60 (Salvia and Ysseldyke 2004). Additionally, the Kuder-Richardson Formula 20 reliability coefficient for the comprehension test is an excellent .93 (MacGinitie et al. 2002).

Validity is the most basic consideration in the development and evaluation of tests (Salvia and Ysseldyke 2004). According to the American Educational Research Association, American Psychological Association, and National Council of Measurement in Education (1999), "Validity refers to the degree to which evidence and theory support the interpretation of test scores entailed by the proposed uses of tests" (p. 9). MacGinitie et al. (2000c) have recommended that the Fourth Edition GMRCT is useful in providing information that will help answer important questions about the reading comprehension of individual students and of groups. Five of the questions proposed by MacGinitie, MacGinitie, Maria, and Dreyer (2000c) are centrally important to this dissertation research project:

1. How well do students as a group read?
2. How well does each student read?
3. How are students as a group progressing?
4. How are individual students progressing in reading?
5. Have interventions made a difference in achievement?

In addition to providing evidence of a sound standardization process and appropriate reliabilities, MacGinitie et al. (2002) supported the validity of utilizing the test results of the GMRCT to help answer the significant questions just listed by providing specific evidence of the test's validity. The author's advanced evidence of content validity, criterion-related validity, and construct validity. MacGinitie et al. (2002) demonstrated that the comprehension test's passages and questions represent the domains of reading comprehension and thus, support the content and construct validity of the GMRCT. Specifically, the passages are a balance of expository and narrative forms intended to represent the varied content that students are required and freely choose to read. The questions are designed to encompass the entire domain of reading comprehension that includes literal and inferential aspects. The test is fashioned to assess the ability of students to employ cognitive strategies to construct meaning from texts.

With respect to criterion-related validity, the GMRCT has been compared with other reading comprehension tests and with the Scholastic Achievement Test Verbal Section. The correlations with both the other reading tests and with the college entrance exam were fairly high (MacGinitie et al. 2002).

The GMRCT was an appropriate means of providing reliable and valid information for this dissertation about individual and group reading achievement levels, individual and group progress in reading, and the possible impact of the instructional intervention on individual and group achievement in reading. The GMRCT has norms based on careful standardization, appropriate reliabilities, and strong content and construct validity. Finally, the GMRCT generates scores and values that can be analyzed to determine the significance of any changes in performance from the pretest to the posttest in this dissertation study. The manner in which the data were utilized by the writer is discussed in the last section of this chapter.

Procedures

The eleventh- and twelfth-grade students participated in a psychology course that included attending to lectures, taking notes, researching, reading texts, reviewing chapters, taking exams, constructing posters, and delivering presentations. The strategic reading intervention was incorporated within the framework of the entire classroom process. The strategic reading process designed for the treatment was a primary means employed by the students to learn the course content. The required textbook provided the bulk of the reading material utilized to learn, practice, and master the specific reading tactics and the entire strategic reading procedure. Supplementary texts that were multicultural in content or appealed to adolescent popular culture were consistently utilized.

Three phases made up the one-group pretest-posttest quantitative research study. The initial phase centered on securing student agreement and parent/guardian consent for participation in the study and administering the study's pretest. The second phase involved the strategic reading treatment. Sixteen weeks were devoted to implementing the two stages of the intervention, the direct instruction and modeling of specific reading tactics, and the strategic reading process as a whole as well as the guided practice and mastery of the reading process. The final phase encompassed the administration of the research project's posttest and analysis of the data. Whereas the posttest was administered in a single class period, many weeks were devoted to interpreting the data and fashioning a report of the findings.

The purpose of the study was to determine the impact of a carefully planned and executed strategic reading process on the reading achievement of a group of high school students enrolled in a psychology class. The vision that provided impetus for the project was that of a classroom of self-motivated and self-regulating students constructing knowledge from texts. The students were foreseen as empowered readers with elevated knowledge/skill resources and motivation.

The classroom climate was envisioned as characterized by (a) warm student-teacher rapport, (b) socially supported learning through cooperative interactions and atmosphere, (c) an exciting curriculum relevant personally and in terms of multicultural popular adolescent culture, and (d) a challenging and serious focus on constructing meaningful knowledge and acquiring reading, thinking, and study skills. The students were envisioned as strengthened because they connected with relevant texts and others in collaborative rapport, had control over their learning through the enhancement of their thinking, study, and reading comprehension competencies; and increased their knowledge base that was fundamental to thinking and fashioning new knowledge.

The specific reading strategies highlighted in the literature review formed the basis of the comprehensive strategic reading process designed for the intervention phase of the study. Five specific reading strategies were integrated into the strategic reading procedure that follows the BDA model promoted by a number of authors (Ogle 1986, Shaw et al. 2000, Vacca and Vacca 2002). The BDA graphic organizer (see Appendix A) is based on the work of numerous educators who have contributed to the development of the BDA strategic reading process.

The first strategy incorporated into the reading process and into the structure of the BDA chart was the KWL technique (Ogle 1986). KWL was utilized when students generated and listed prior knowledge and questions on the chart before reading and when questions were answered while reading.

The second reading tactic integrated into the reading process of the intervention and into the BDA chart's workings was SQ3R. SQ3R was employed during the prereading stage when students were asked to preview the assigned reading and to formulate questions that might be answered during reading (Johns and Lenski 2001).

Reciprocal reading was the third specific reading strategy included in the reading process and within the structure of the BDA chart. While reading, students were asked to self-regulate engagement with texts by questioning, summarizing, clarifying, and predicting (Alfassi 2004).

The fourth technique utilized in the treatment's comprehensive reading procedure was strategic vocabulary study (Fisher 2001, Johns and Lenski 2001). Understanding vocabulary to construct knowledge more effectively from texts was stressed throughout the reading process and included in each of the three divisions of the BDA chart.

The final reading strategy incorporated in the instructional intervention was structured note-taking (Shaw et al. 2000, Vacca and Vacca 2002). Making notes is an excellent means of promoting self-regulated reading and of organizing important information.

The focal point of instruction and learning to master the strategic reading process was the BDA chart. The processes that empower readers to process information and construct knowledge more efficiently were embedded in the procedures required when utilizing the chart. Instruction, modeling, and scaffolding were supplied by a more expert reader. The collaborative and interactive nature of the learning activities entailed in mastery of the chart's use provided for the social mediation of learning. The reader's solitary task of internalizing the strategic reading process was supported by the instruction, modeling, and encouragement of others.

Following is a week-by-week account of the study's procedures that actualized the research design of this applied dissertation. Daily activities for the first stage of the treatment phase of the study are reported. The writer believed that, for the study to be replicated, a day-to-day accounting of the instruction and modeling initially afforded the students, and later provided throughout the intervention phase, was necessary.

Week one. The writer met with the parents and guardians of the students. The appropriate permission forms were read, and the study was explained. The writer answered questions that the students and the adults raised. Twenty-two students, with family approval, agreed to be part of the research project. One student told the writer that he preferred not to participate. The student was assured that his decision would not affect the instruction he received or treatment in class. As required by school district policy, the pupil who was not part of the study group received the same educational programming, including the strategic reading instruction, that classmates received. The student was a fully participating student in the class, with the exception of being exempted from the study's pretest and posttest.

Week two. On day one, Level 10/12 Form S of the GMRCT was administered to the twenty-two students in the study. The students were given thirty-five minutes to answer the forty-eight questions that addressed the eleven selections comprising the test. The writer carefully read the instructions to the class supplied by MacGinitie et al. (2000b) and closely monitored the students during testing. Each student created a code name that was utilized to disassociate actual student names and tests and match the pretest with the posttest that was administered sixteen weeks later. Tests were corrected by the writer and stored in a locked cabinet in a colleague's office.

On day two, forty minutes of the eighty-minute learning block were focused on presenting the BDA chart and providing an overview of its purpose and use in supplying a means of increasing reading comprehension and of learning the content of the psychology course. After answering questions that the students had, the writer introduced the topic of the next section of the psychology text with a short phrase. The class and teacher brainstormed to compose a list of the group's current knowledge of the topic. The writer listed the ideas on the board under a "My Knowledge" heading. The students were then asked to select from the list items that they believed were relevant and to list these ideas on their BDA charts.

Next, the teacher and the class surveyed the reading selection. Students and teacher took turns reading the headings, captions, and boldface vocabulary and definitions. The students and the teacher next generated questions regarding what they thought they would learn or what they wanted to learn by reading the selection. The teacher listed the questions on the board under a "My Questions" heading. Students were then asked to select two or three questions that they found interesting and to copy them on their charts. The students and teacher then took turns reading the section of the textbook. The learning session concluded with the teacher summarizing the lesson and answering questions.

On day three, the forty-minutes of the block set aside for reading instruction started with a question-and-answer session, centered on the understanding the group had of the BDA chart's use. Students were asked about their views concerning the value of reflecting on current knowledge of a topic and formulating questions before reading. After a brief discussion, the teacher repeated the process of the previous day while utilizing the next section of the psychology textbook. Prior knowledge was elicited and questions formulated. Students completed the appropriate areas of the chart. Before orally reading the selection, the teacher directed attention of the class to the board where the following was written: (a) questioning, (b) summarizing, (c) clarifying, and (d) predicting.

The teacher then engaged the class in a discussion about how these practices might help a reader to focus and learn more by reading. The teacher and the class next read the section. The readers were asked to pause at the end of one or two paragraphs, and the teacher modeled questioning, summarizing, clarifying, and predicting. Questions that were created before reading were discussed when answers appeared in the passages. The lesson ended with the teacher supplying a summary and answering questions.

On day four, the pattern established so far was followed. The textbook again supplied the text utilized in the process of eliciting the group's prior knowledge of a topic and generating questions to foster purposeful reading. The teacher modeled questioning, summarizing, clarifying, and predicting during oral reading. Students were directed to record answers to any of their questions, uncovered during the reading, on their charts.

On day five, the thirty-five minutes reserved for instruction on the reading techniques, the BDA chart focused on the notes section of the chart. While a selection from the psychology textbook was being read aloud, the teacher modeled taking appropriate notes. Students were asked to record the notes in the space provided on the chart. The teacher emphasized the importance of noting terms and definitions. The session drew to a close with a discussion of how actively reading enhances making notes.

Week three. On day one, the strategies of generating prior knowledge, posting questions, answering questions, and making notes were applied to a section of the course textbook. After the before and during sections of the BDA chart were completed at the conclusion of oral reading, the students received the Concept Mapping graphic organizer (see Appendix B). The teacher demonstrated the use of the graphic organizer by constructing three concept maps utilizing the terms found in the sections of the textbook that were previously read. The teacher guided a discussion of the maps that were displayed on the board. Finally, the teacher illustrated how an understanding of terms helps to construct knowledge of the text. The lesson concluded with an opportunity for students to ask questions.

On day two, the thirty-five-minute strategic reading lesson focused on the structured note-taking technique. Once again, the psychology textbook supplied the reading material and students learned course content while being introduced to a valuable reading/study tactic. While the students examined the Structured Notes graphic organizer (see Appendix C), the teacher explained and modeled its use. The students were guided to an understanding that the notes that were created reflected the structure of the section's headings and subheadings. A concluding discussion highlighted the importance of including unfamiliar terms and definitions in notes.

On day three, forty minutes were devoted to the collaborative learning of the strategic reading process. The teacher had arranged the class into cooperative learning groups of three or four students prior to the learning session. After the teacher introduced the topic of the reading from the psychology textbook with a short phrase, each group discussed prior knowledge, and each student completed the "My Knowledge" section of the BDA chart. Each group then previewed the reading selection, and after a discussion, each group member listed questions on the chart.

Next, the section was read by volunteers from the various groups. The students were asked to question, summarize, clarify, and predict during the times of transition between the volunteer oral readers. Students were additionally asked to make notes during the pauses. At the conclusion of the reading, each student was directed to check "Structured Notes" in the after reading section of the chart. Finally, the groups were asked to divide the passages just read among the group members, with each student making notes for his or her part. The groups were instructed to save the notes for the next day's class.

On day four, the final day of direct instruction and modeling was given to creating a written summary of the selection read the previous day. Students were first asked to check "Written Summary" in the after section of the BDA chart. Each group member was then directed to use his or her notes from the previous day to write a summary. The group then collaboratively fashioned the individual summaries into a group composition that summarized the reading from the day before. The teacher monitored the groups and scaffold the learning as needed. The session ended with oral presentations of the group compositions and a class discussion focused on good summarizing.

On day five, forty minutes were set aside for teacher-student discussions. While the group worked on poster or research projects, the teacher met with individual students to gain insights into their understandings and needs. The teacher made a point of encouraging and appropriately praising the achievements demonstrated through class participation and that were documented on the BDA charts.

Week four. The second stage of the treatment phase of this dissertation study began at the beginning of the fourth week. Thirty to forty minutes of the eighty-minute learning block were employed for guided practice of the reading techniques and utilizing the BDA chart to learn the psychology course content. The first four days of lessons focused on the cognitive strategies of questioning, summarizing, clarifying, and predicting. A comprehension quiz was administered, involving ten questions covering the content of three short passages in the psychology textbook. Students were required to employ both literal and inferential comprehension skills. Whereas some questions entailed the recall of information explicitly stated in the selections, other questions required analysis, synthesis, or evaluation. The last day of the week was scheduled for short student-teacher conferences. The writer utilized the time to encourage individual students and to provide individualized instruction as needed. The teacher actively promoted warm student-teacher rapport.

Week five. The prereading tactics of generating prior knowledge of topics, surveying selections, and creating questions for purposeful reading were stressed throughout the week. Students were presented an article relevant to adolescent life and were asked to independently complete the BDA chart, including the making of structured notes. A comprehension quiz was administered the following day. Students were encouraged to utilize the notes they had made the previous day to help them answer the questions. The teacher collected and graded the charts and quizzes. Individual comments on the quality of notes were provided to each student by the teacher. The teacher provided scaffolding tailored to individual needs.

Week six. Students worked cooperatively throughout the week. The concentration of the strategic reading segment of the learning block was on developing skill in understanding vocabulary and utilizing vocabulary knowledge to construct better meaning from texts. Throughout the week, the collaborative learning groups created concept maps covering the terms in the readings from the course textbook and from a number of articles that the teacher provided. The supplementary reading materials were multicultural and popular culture in theme.

Week seven. The emphasis of the week was on structured note-taking. The process was reviewed and discussed. Students were required to read a section of the psychology textbook and independently complete the BDA chart. After checking the appropriate option in the after section of the chart, the students began making notes while reading. The students completed the assignment for homework and were administered a comprehension test the following day. The teacher met with individual students on the final day of the week. Once again, the teacher endeavored to build rapport, encourage, and provide individualized instruction.

Week eight. During daily lectures on the psychology curriculum and while discussing assigned readings, the teacher challenged students to think more deeply. The teacher modeled and encouraged students to analyze, synthesize, evaluate, and apply while listening and reading. The teacher guided students to higher-level thinking through questions that required such processes. Students were invited to apply the thinking strategies to what they heard and read during the week.

Week nine. The cooperative learning groups worked together to fashion structured notes. The teacher was conscious of the need to allow for the social support of individual learning and for modeling supplied by peers. After completing a set of notes, the students were presented a ten-point comprehension quiz. The assessment required responses involving recall and higher-level thinking. The charts and quizzes were returned with constructive comments the following day.

Week ten. During the week, students worked both in cooperative learning groups and independently in fashioning written summaries of reading selections. The teacher provided writing prompts to ensure that the summaries included analysis, synthesis, evaluation, and application. The textbook readings were supplemented by an article that focused on popular culture.

Week eleven. The strategic reading portion of the daily learning block fully focused on utilizing effective reading to master the psychology course content scheduled for the week. The teacher reiterated the importance of self-regulated reading achieved by questioning, summarizing, clarifying, and predicting while engaged with a text. The teacher modeled the techniques while reading several paragraphs from the course textbook. Students were required to read a significant portion of a chapter, complete the BDA chart independently, and make structured notes. The group was tested and the charts and quizzes graded. The teacher returned the corrected charts and quizzes with instructive and encouraging comments.

Week twelve. The emphasis during the daily thirty-five minutes scheduled time for reading practice and learning by reading was on cooperatively constructing concept maps. The teacher was conscious of the need to structure socially mediated learning and monitored the progress of the cooperative learning groups throughout the week. It was not necessary for the teacher to model the process of creating effective concept maps. The groups of students were able to create excellent visual representations of the relationships among the important terms in the chapter being studied.

Week thirteen. The instructional objectives for the week, with respect to the strategic reading process, were to evaluate the extent to which the students had mastered the use of the BDA chart. Because the proper utilization of the chart entailed the proper use of the strategies that constitute the strategic reading process, the teacher was evaluating the mastery of the process.

Students were asked to call to mind independently prior knowledge about topics, preview assigned sections of the textbook, and formulate questions. While reading, the students were asked to self-monitor by questioning, summarizing, clarifying, and predicting. The students made notes during extended periods of silent reading. On the day following the reading of a large part of a chapter, the students were tested. Following the established practice, the teacher graded charts and quizzes and returned the documents with comments to the students.

Week fourteen. During this week, students worked within their cooperative learning groups. After reading assigned selections from the textbook and articles provided by the teacher, the students compared the notes they had taken with group members.

Week fifteen. The objective of the week regarding the strategic reading process was to have students create quality summaries by utilizing notes that they made. The teacher provided a lengthy article that had a multicultural theme. After reading the article and taking notes, the students were given a writing prompt. The prompt required a summary that involved analyzing, synthesizing, and evaluating. The remainder of the time set aside for reading during the week was devoted to promoting the habit of self-regulated reading. Students were assigned short passages from the psychology textbook together with three questions to answer. Because only three to five minutes were allotted for reading the passages and answering the questions, the students were encouraged to self-monitor fully.

Week sixteen. The higher-order thinking skills were the focus throughout the week. The teacher intentionally and consistently formulated thought-provoking questions during oral reading of textbook and articles and after student or teacher presentations. The questions required the analysis, synthesis, evaluation, and application of information. Throughout the week, the students were given short passages to read along with questions to answer within limited time frames. The objective here was to stimulate a habit of self-regulated reading.

Week seventeen. The treatment or instructional intervention phase of the study was concluded by midweek. The students utilized the BDA chart for the final time while reading an article that was multicultural and popular culture in theme. The posttest was administered at midweek so as to avoid a conflict, with two days set aside for final exam review. The teacher carefully adhered to the guidelines outlined by MacGinitie, MacGinitie, Maria, and Dreyer (2000b) for administering the GMRCT (Form T, Level 10/12). The teacher corrected the tests and secured all test materials in a locked cabinet.

Data Analysis and Reporting Plan

The purpose of the applied dissertation study was to determine the impact of reading strategies instruction in a psychology class on reading comprehension achievement. The research data focused on the study's purpose and on a single research question, will students receiving reading strategies instruction in a content-area class realize statistically significant and educationally meaningful gains in reading comprehension achievement?

A one-group, pretest-posttest design was selected for the study rather than a true experimental design with treatment and comparison groups. The school district where the research was conducted does not permit research involving differential instruction to students. Although the one-group nature of the study limits the ability to determine the impact of the reading intervention on the reading comprehension achievement of the participating students, the research question may be fully answered through statistical procedures applied to pretest and posttest data. In a more limited way, evidence can be advanced to address the purpose statement of the study.

The plan for analyzing and reporting the data included utilizing normal curve equivalents (NCEs) from the standardized GMRCT to compare the performance of the students in the study with the norming group of the standardized instrument. On the basis of the comparative analysis, the writer formulated conclusions about the impact of the reading instruction on the reading comprehension achievement of the group as a whole, on subgroups, and on individual students.

The data analysis and reporting plan entailed five requirements: (a) presentation of descriptive statistics, (b) report on a test to determine the statistical significance of the findings, (c) report on a procedure that determines the educational meaningfulness of the results, (d) presentation of data that addresses the study's purpose of determining the impact of the instruction on reading comprehension achievement, and (e) interpretation and discussion of the meaning of the findings. The first four requirements are accomplished in the following chapter, whereas the final demand is met in the concluding chapter.

The presentation of descriptive statistics centered on raw scores initiates the results report in the first section of the chapter on results. The report provides the data necessary for the statistical procedures that determine statistical significance and educational meaningfulness of the findings for the group as a whole and for the gender and racial subgroups identified in the study. The dependent *t* test is the appropriate test for determining the statistical significance of any observed change in achievement from pretest to posttest in a one-group study. The appropriate equal interval scale score is the raw score (S. D. Griffin, personal communication, November 2, 2005).

Because the dependent *t* test compares the means from the same group and is most often used to analyze pretest and posttest data, the descriptive data report features pretest and posttest raw score means and raw score difference means (difference between pretest and posttest means). The same means are necessary to the Cohen's *d* procedure used in this study to determine the educational meaningfulness of any observed change in reading comprehension performance from pretest to posttest. Raw score is, again, the appropriate equal interval scale score to utilize (S. D. Griffin, personal communication, November 2, 2005).

The first section of the chapter, reporting results, continues with a presentation of the findings of the two inferential statistical procedures. The dependent *t* test results are first set forth, followed by the conclusions of the Cohen's *d* procedure.

The statistical significance of any observed changes in performance for the study group as a whole and for gender and racial subgroups are calculated through utilization of the dependent *t* test. A *t*-statistic is determined by entering the pretest and posttest raw score means into the Statistical Package for Social Studies 12.0 (SPSS 12.0) for Windows Student Version program. Consistent with the customary practice, a mean difference score of a magnitude that results in a *t*-statistic at a probability value of .05 represents a change unlikely due to chance or a large discrepancy between means and is statistically significant (S. D. Griffin, personal communication, November 2, 2005). A probability value of .05 ($p = .05$) is the cutoff to evaluate results.

After the matter of statistical significance has been addressed, the first section of the next chapter concludes by addressing the second requirement of the research question. Cohen's *d* procedure was applied to the pretest and posttest mean data to ascertain whether any observed increase in reading achievement for the group as a whole or for any identified subgroup was educationally meaningful.

Probability value does not tell anything about how large a difference was observed. As sample size increases, probability values get smaller. Therefore, it is possible that a trivial difference between groups or between means of the same group is statistically significant and that an important difference is not. Because of the concern with probability values, it is widely recommended that measures of effect size be reported with probability values (S. D. Griffin, personal communication, November 2, 2005).

This applied dissertation's writer was centrally interested in the educational or practical meaningfulness of any observed difference in reading achievement from pretest to posttest. Cohen's *d* procedure is an effect size measure used to compare the means of two groups or two means from the same group. The effect size is calculated by multiplying the *t*-statistic by two and dividing the product by the square root of the number of participants minus one. The resulting value represents a quantified magnitude of a difference in means not influenced by sample size. Cohen's *d* measures how different two mean scores are relative to standard deviation units. The effect size measure tells how many standard deviation units apart the two means are.

Once Cohen's *d* is calculated by comparing this study's pretest and posttest means, the educational meaningfulness of any observed gains in achievement can be determined. The following criteria are employed to evaluate the *d* statistic: (a) *d* = .20 (one-fifth of a standard deviation) is a small effect size, (b) *d* = .50 (one half of a standard deviation) is a medium effect size, (c) *d* = .80 (eight-tenth of a standard deviation) is a large effect size (S. D. Griffin, personal communication, November 2, 2005). For the purpose of this dissertation, a Cohen's *d* > .80 would indicate an educationally meaningful gain in reading comprehension.

The second section of the following chapter on results supplies the data necessary to address the dissertation's purpose statement. The data focus on the NCE scores of the group as a whole, of the subgroups, and of particular students with significant NCE difference scores from pretest to posttest. A number of tables support the narrative report.

The second equal interval scale score featured in the descriptive data is, then, the NCE score. NCEs are derived scores obtained from the raw scores on the GMRCT. Derived scores enhance interpretation by supplying a quantitative measure of each student's performance relative to the norming group (Gall, Gall, and Borg 2003). MacGinitie et al. (2000c) suggested using NCEs "when differences between a student's score from testing to testing are to be interpreted" (p. 37). MacGinitie et al. (2000c) also proposed using NCE scores "when differences between a group's score from testing to testing are to be interpreted" (p. 35). The second section, therefore, presents data concerning the NCE means of the entire group and subgroups, as well as data on the mean NCE difference scores.

In addition, the report details the number and percentages of students by group and subgroups who had (a) positive difference scores (posttest score > pretest score), (b) zero difference scores (posttest score = pretest score), and (c) negative difference scores (posttest score < pretest score). During the account of difference scores, a number of individual scores within the various subgroups are highlighted. These scores significantly impacted the mean scores of the group as a whole and of the relevant subgroups. In addition, large positive difference scores provide evidence of the impact of the reading instruction on the reading achievement of the students, who achieved the large increase in scores from pretest to posttest.

NCEs, like percentile ranks, describe a student's level of achievement relative to the achievement of other students in the same grade. NCEs are, in fact, percentile ranks statistically transformed into equal interval units of reading achievement. Since NCEs are equal scale units, NCEs are appropriate for comparing pretests and posttest means. In addition, NCEs are appropriate for assessing the progress of individual students and groups from testing to testing compared with the norming group (MacGinitie et al., 2000c).

MacGinitie et al. (2000c) established criteria for evaluating the progress of a student and a group by utilizing NCEs to compare the individual or group score with the norming group. In a one-group study with a pretest and posttest, such as the one in this dissertation, the norming group can serve as a comparison group (Semel and Wiig 1981). However, MacGinitie et al. (2000c) cautioned that the NCE difference score (comparing pretest and posttest scores) is not a perfect indicator of the student's or group's performance relative to the group used to standardize the test. Caution must be exercised in drawing conclusions from NCE difference scores. Only large NCE difference scores most likely indicate that the individual or group progressed at a faster rate than expected based on the data of the norming group.

Therefore, only large NCE difference scores are considered evidence for the impact of this study's treatment on any observed increases in reading comprehension achievement. Consistent with the practice established by Semel and Wiig, the writer's data plan entailed formulating a large estimate of the magnitude of NCE difference scores that counted as indicators of larger-than-expected gains in reading achievement. These large difference scores may be considered as possible evidence for the impact of reading strategies instruction on the reading achievement. For the Gates-MacGinitie Reading Tests that include both vocabulary and comprehension tests, MacGinitie et al. (2000c) found that a mean NCE difference score of 2.2 indicated, at a probability level of 0.05, that the group realized some relative growth in achievement.

For the individual score, the authors established a difference score of 4.0, at a probability of 0.15, as the cutoff for evaluating results. On the basis of the criteria set forth by MacGinitie et al. (2000c), the writer's data plan set the scores for evaluating progress relative to the norming group at demanding levels of 4.4 (4.4 percentiles) for group mean NCE difference scores and 8.0 (8.0 percentiles) for individual difference scores. The writer's plan maintained that NCE mean increases of 4.4 or greater for a group and of 8.0 NCEs or greater for an individual over the four months between the study's pretest and posttest were large and would be considered as evidence of the impact of reading strategies instruction on the reading achievement of the group or individual of concern.

In conclusion, the one-group research design significantly inhibits efforts to answer the study's purpose statement. However, some evidence may be gathered by considering any (a) large NCE difference scores, (b) statistically significant increase in achievement by the study group and/or subgroups, and (c) educationally significant gains realized by the entire group and/or subgroups. The writer's data analysis and reporting plan intended to focus attention on these three sources of information. Conversely, the task of answering the dual requirements of the research question may be directly discharged. The two statistical tests discussed above were utilized to determine the statistical significance and educational meaningfulness of the findings.

CHAPTER 4

Results

This chapter is organized into two sections. The first addresses the requirements of the research question to determine whether any observed increases in reading comprehension were statistically significant and educationally meaningful. The descriptive data bearing on the research question are presented first. The presentation then continues with a report of the results of two statistical procedures utilized to answer the question that guided the design and implementation of the research project.

The second part of the report provides additional data intended to address this dissertation's purpose of assessing the impact of the reading strategies instruction on the reading comprehension achievement of the participating students. Descriptive data centered on NCE scores, NCE means, and NCE difference scores are presented. Attention is then turned to evaluating the scores and means by the criteria established in the data plan section of the previous chapter.

Data are provided to summarize the findings on (a) the statistical significance of any observed increases in reading comprehension achievement from pretest to posttest, (b) the educational importance of any observed increases in performance, and (c) the evidence of the impact of the strategic reading intervention based on study group and norming group comparisons. These data include the results of the group as a whole and of the gender and racial subgroups.

Raw Score Data and Statistical Tests

Twenty-two students participated in the research study. The psychology class was composed of ten females and six males of White American background, and two females and four males of African American heritage.

Ten students in the study group realized positive difference scores or had increases in raw scores from pretest to posttest. Seven students had zero difference scores or scored the same on the pretest and posttest. Five students had negative difference scores or score decreases. The study group had a pretest mean score of 35.18 on the forty-eight-question comprehension test and a posttest average score of 37.18. The mean difference score was 2.00.

In the female subgroup, seven students attained positive difference scores. Whereas three of the students scored the same on the pretest and the posttest, two scored lower on the posttest than on the pretest. The female group's pretest mean was 34.66, and the posttest mean was 38.08. This group's mean difference score was 3.42.

Three of the ten students in the male subgroup earned positive difference scores; four had identical pretest and posttest scores, and three decreased in performance from pretest to posttest. The pretest and posttest mean scores for the male subgroup were 35.80 and 36.10 respectively. The mean difference score for this subgroup was 0.30.

Data for the racial subgroups were disaggregated from the group as a whole. Eight of sixteen White American students attained positive difference scores; six of these students had no change in score from pretest to posttest, and two had decreased scores. The pretest mean score for the White American students was 36.75, and the posttest average score was 39.31. The mean difference score for this group was 2.56.

Two of the students in the African American subgroup realized positive difference scores, three did not change in score from pretest to posttest, and one student scored less on the posttest than on the pretest. The pretest and posttest means for the African American students were 31.00 and 31.50 respectively. This subgroup's mean difference score was 0.50.

Data were also disaggregated from the total group regarding the performance of racial-gender subgroups. Six of ten White females achieved positive difference scores; three had identical scores on the pretest and the posttest, and one decreased in achievement. The White American female subgroup had a pretest mean score of 35.40 and a posttest score of 38.90. This subgroup's mean difference score was 3.50.

In the White American male subgroup of six students, two earned positive difference scores; three scored the same on the pretest and posttest, and one decreased in achievement. The pretest and posttest mean scores for the White American male subgroup were 39.00 and 40.00 respectively. This group's mean difference score was 1.00.

The African American female subgroup had two members. One student increased in score from pretest to posttest, and the other experienced a decline in performance. The two students combined for a pretest mean of 31.00 and a posttest mean score of 34.00. The mean difference score for the African American females was 3.00.

Among the four members of the African American male subgroup, one student realized a positive difference score. Another student maintained the same score from pretest to posttest, and the remaining students in this group declined in measured achievement. The pretest and posttest mean scores for the African American males were 31.00 and 30.25 respectively. The mean difference score for this subgroup was -0.75.

The descriptive data report focused on raw score difference scores and raw score mean difference scores. These scores are necessary to address the research question requirements. Following are the results of the two statistical procedures utilized in this study to determine the statistical significance and educational meaningfulness of any observed increases in reading comprehension achievement.

Determining statistical significance: The dependent t test. The dependent *t* test was used to determine the statistical significance of the observed gains in reading performance. The pretest and posttest means for the group as a whole and for subgroups that attained increases in mean scores were analyzed by utilizing SPSS 12.0. The customary criteria of p < .05 was used to evaluate the results.

Of the seven subgroups that achieved gains in reading comprehension performance, four had insignificant increases. The male subgroup mean difference score or score increase was 0.30. The results of the *t* test were *t* = 0.326, *sig.* (two-tailed) = .752. This subgroup's gain in achievement was not significant. Next, the African American subgroup's mean score increase was 0.50. The results of the *t* test were *t* = 0.289, *sig.* (two-tailed) = .789. The improvement of this group was not significant. Third, White American males realized a mean difference score of 1.00. The *t* test results were *t* = 1.000, *sig.* (two-tailed) = .363. The gain in achievement of the White American male subgroup was not significant. Finally, the two African American females attained a mean gain of 3.00. The *t* test outcomes were *t* = .750, *sig.* (two-tailed) = .590.

The study group as a whole, as well as the three largest subgroups, realized statistically significant gains in reading. These results bear importantly on the interpretation of findings shown in the next chapter. Table 1 highlights the results of the analysis for the total group and the subgroups that achieved significant reading comprehension improvements.

Determining educational meaningfulness: Cohen's d test. In order to meet the research question's demand to determine the practical or educational importance of the observed gains in achievement, Cohen's d effect size test was employed. The criterion for evaluating results was established as d > .80.

Table 1
Statistically Significant Achievement Increases

Group	*N*	MDS	*t*	*p*
All participants	22	2.00	2.381	.027
Females	12	3.42	2.797	.017
White Americans	16	2.56	2.689	.017
White American females	10	3.50	2.589	.029

Note. MDS = mean difference score. A statistically significant MDS has a *p* < .05.

Of the seven subgroups that realized achievement gains in reading comprehension performance, two had increases that were not educationally meaningful. First, the male subgroup's mean score increase was 0.30. The result of the Cohen's *d* test was *d* = 0.22. The 0.22 standard deviation difference between pretest and posttest mean scores was not educationally meaningful. Second, the African American subgroup had a 0.50 mean score improvement. The result of the Cohen's *d* test was *d* = 0.26. The 0.26 standard deviation difference between pretest and posttest mean scores was not educationally important.

The study group as a whole, as well as five subgroups, had educationally meaningful improvements in reading comprehension achievement. The mean difference scores and the effect sizes for the total group and the five subgroups are reported in Table 2. The large effect sizes ranged from a 0.89 standard deviation difference between pretest and posttest means to a 1.73 standard deviation difference. Owing to the importance of the data to the interpretation of the study's results, the findings for educationally meaningful achievement increases are presented.

Table 2

Educationally Meaningful Achievement Increases

Group	N	MDS	d
All participants	22	2.00	1.04
Females	12	3.42	1.69
White Americans	16	2.56	1.39
White American females	10	3.50	1.73
White American males	6	1.00	0.89
African American females	2	3.00	1.50

Note. MDS = mean difference score. An educationally meaningful MDS has a Cohen's $d > 0.80$.

The Intervention's Impact: Comparing Study and Norming Groups

NCEs were utilized in this section to provide the data necessary to evaluate evidence of the impact of the reading instruction on the observed gains in reading achievement. The lack of a comparison group, which would have controlled for such factors as maturation, limited the ability to correlate the reading treatment and the achievement outcomes in this one-group study. This limitation could be, in part, overcome by utilizing scores derived from the raw scores as a basis for reporting findings. An alternate comparison group emerged when NCEs, or percentile ranks of reading achievement, were utilized. The data were then compared to the data of the standardized test's norming group.

The writer's data analysis and reporting plan called for establishing high estimates of NCE difference scores as evidence of the effect of the treatment on the observed gains in performance. The NCE difference scores, or changes in scores from pretest to posttest, that were defined to evaluate the performance of the study's students and groups relative to the performance of the norming group were 8.0 percentiles for individual scores and 4.4 percentiles for group mean scores.

The report of the findings focused on the group as a whole and the eight subgroups: female, male, White American, African American, (e) White American females, (f) White American males, (g) African American females, and (h) African American males. Each presentation begins by reporting the number of students in each category who realized greater than expected achievement or had positive NCE difference scores, maintained the same level of performance from pretest to posttest or had zero difference scores, and declined in achievement or had negative NCE difference scores. Then, the number of students in each category that surpassed the 8.0 percentile criterion level of improvement is listed. Finally, NCE pretest and posttest means and the resulting NCE mean difference scores are presented.

Fourteen of the twenty-two students in the study realized higher-than-expected scores on the posttest or had NCE difference scores greater than zero. Four students progressed at the same rate as peers in the norming group or had NCE difference scores of zero. The four remaining students had lower than expected scores on the posttest. These students had negative NCE difference scores. Eight students realized large improvements in performance ranging from eleven to twenty-nine percentiles or NCEs. These scores may be counted as evidence of the positive effect of the intervention on the observed achievement improvements. The total group had an NCE mean of 65.41 on the pretest and a 71.82 mean on the posttest. The group, as a whole, surpassed the criterion established for NCE mean percentile gains and therefore, provided evidence of the positive impact of the reading treatment on the observed increase in performance. The findings for the total group are presented in Table 3.

Table 3
Evidence of Intervention's Effect on Achievement Gains

Group	N	NCEMDS
All participants	22	6.41
Females	12	9.95
White Americans	16	8.75
White American females	10	10.80
White American males	6	5.33
African Americans females	2	4.50

Note. NCEMDS = normal curve equivalent mean difference score. Evidence of the intervention's effect is a NCEMDS > 4.40.

Among the twelve students in the female subgroup, nine improved in percentile rank from pretest to posttest or had positive NCE difference scores. Whereas one student's percentile rank remained the same, indicating that she progressed as expected compared with peers in the norming group, two female students fell in percentile standing from pretest to posttest. Five of the female subgroup's members had large improvements in achievement of over 8.0 percentiles. The female students combined for pretest and posttest NCE means of 63.75 and 73.50 respectively. In exceeding the 4.40 mean percentile gain criterion, the female subgroup's results may be considered as evidence of the intervention's influence on the observed improvement.

Five of the ten males in the study realized greater-than-expected performance gains as measured on the NCE percentile scale. Whereas three male students progressed as expected with NCE difference scores of zero, two declined in achievement. Two were among the eight students who realized large improvements of over 8.00 percentiles. The pretest NCE mean for the male subgroup was 67.40, and the posttest mean was 69.80. The 2.40 NCE mean difference score did not meet the criterion for a large gain in performance.

Twelve members of the White American subgroup attained performance gains beyond what was expected compared with the norming group. Three subgroup members maintained the same percentile rank from pretest to posttest and one student declined in percentile score. The White American subgroup included 7 of the 8 students that achieved large performance increases of over 8.0 percentiles. The pretest and posttest NCE means for this subgroup were 69.00 and 77.75. The NCE mean percentile gain surpassed the 4.4 standard set for determining large achievement increases. The findings for the White American subgroup may be considered as evidence of the positive impact of the treatment on the observed improvement (see Table 3).

Of the six students in the African American subgroup, two achieved increases in performance, one maintained the same percentile rank, and three declined in achievement level from pretest to posttest. One of the subgroup members had a large improvement increase of over 8.0 percentiles. The pretest NCE mean for the African American subgroup was 55.83, and the posttest mean was 56.00. The 0.17 mean NCE difference score or percentile increase was small.

Eight of the ten White American females attained larger-than-expected gains in reading comprehension achievement. One of the members of this subgroup maintained her percentile performance rank from pretest to posttest, and one experienced an achievement decline. Of the eight students in the study who realized large improvements of over 8.0 percentiles, five were in the White American female subgroup. The pretest and posttest NCE means for this group were 65.30 and 76.10 respectively. The White American female subgroup attained a large performance improvement. The data for this subgroup are shown in Table 3.

Four of the six White American males achieved performance gains beyond what was expected based on a comparison with the norming group. The other two maintained their ninety-ninth percentile level of achievement. Two of the eight students in the study who achieved improvements greater than 8.0 percentiles were in the White American male subgroup. The pretest NCE mean score for this subgroup was 75.17, and the posttest average was 80.50. The White American male subgroup exceeded the NCE mean 4.4 criterion for a large improvement that may give evidence of the impact of the reading intervention on observed gains in reading performance. The data for this group are highlighted in Table 3.

One of the two African American females was among the eight students in the study who increased in reading performance from pretest to posttest beyond 8.0 percentiles. The other decreased in measured achievement. The pretest NCE mean for the African American subgroup was 56.00, and the posttest average was 60.50. The mean percentile improvement of this group surpassed the

4.4 standard and indicate the treatment's impact on performance increases. Table 3 contains the results for this group regarding evidence of intervention influence on reading performance.

One member of the African American male subgroup realized an NCE performance gain, and another maintained the same percentile level of achievement from pretest to posttest. The other two declined in measured achievement. The pretest and posttest NCE means for the African American male subgroup were 55.75 and 53.75 respectively. This subgroup had a negative difference score or decreased 2.0 percentiles from pretest to posttest.

As mentioned, Table 3 highlights the total group and subgroup findings that may be considered in the next chapter's interpretation of results as evidence for the impact of the study's intervention on the observed increases in reading achievement. The information presented in Table 3, as well as the data regarding large percentile gains in performance realized by individual students, are discussed in chapter 5.

CHAPTER 5

Discussion

Overview of the Applied Dissertation

A CONCERN COMPELLED THE WRITER to develop and carry out a study focused on determining the impact of strategic reading instruction on the reading comprehension achievement of a group of high school students. The concern was generated by the writer's awareness of three conditions. First, the overall reading achievement of the school's students had been at an unacceptably low level for some time. About 50 percent of the freshman class tested two or more grade levels below grade nine since the 2003–2004 school year. The problem has persisted through the eleventh grade according to available data. Approximately 50 percent of the junior class scored below proficiency in reading on the latest state assessment.

Second, research indicated that strategic reading instruction was effective in elevating the reading performance of high school students (Alfassi 2004, Fisher 2001, Frey, Lee, Tallefson, Pass, and Massengill 2005; Myers and Savage 2005, Quiocho 1997, Slater and Horstman 2002, Vacca and Vacca 2002).

Third, the high school of concern did not provide consistent and widespread strategic reading instruction for students. The high school where this dissertation's study took place, along with the vast majority of secondary schools in the United States, are not well informed regarding the value of reading instruction in bolstering the reading capabilities of secondary students (Alfassi, Slater and Horstman, Vacca and Vacca).

The intent of the research project was to contribute to the amelioration of the reading achievement problem at the high school. The purpose of implementing the reading intervention, collecting data, and conducting an analysis was to determine the impact of the instruction on the reading achievement of one psychology class. The writer endeavored to provide thorough strategic reading instruction to ensure that reading became a central means of learning the course content and mastering the reading tactics resulted in reading achievement gains.

In addition to instructing, modeling, and guiding the reading process, the writer was conscious of the necessity to sustain the classroom climate that supported the development of the skills and habits necessary to read efficiently. The climate was characterized by high expectations and the respect, discipline, and helping hand that Reglin (1995) found to be essential to foster the achievement of diverse groups of students. In order to heighten motivation and to connect all students with reading texts, supplementary assigned readings were multicultural and popular culture in content.

Underpinning the learning process and the classroom climate was an ethic of care. The writer found that Wilder (1999) was correct in concluding that students exert extra effort when they feel cared about by teachers. The underlying assumption of this dissertation's study was realized in practice. The interactive and collaborative manner in which reading strategies were taught and learned significantly contributed to a supportive classroom environment. Students found support for the solitary task of internalizing the reading strategies that increase the ability to construct knowledge from texts.

The writer's primary interest during the one-group, pretest-posttest study was to benefit this group of psychology students. The treatment phase of the research project was given to ensure that the learning process provided genuine opportunities for each learner to master the course content and the strategic reading process. At the conclusion of the intervention phase, attention centered on the analysis of data gathered through the tests. The analysis intended to address the study's purpose and to answer the research question. The results that answer the requirements of the study's research question are reported first. Then, the findings that address the study's purpose are presented.

The research question set forth two requirements that the data analysis needed to address. The question asked, will students receiving reading strategies instruction in a content-area class realize statistically significant and educationally meaningful gains in reading comprehension achievement?

To begin with, the group, as a whole, realized both statistically significant and educationally meaningful increases in reading comprehension achievement. In addition, three of eight subgroups achieved statistically significant gains in reading, and five of the subgroups had educationally important increases.

The task of addressing the study's purpose of determining the impact of the strategic reading instruction on reading comprehension made necessary the utilization of a derived score from the standardized test. Because the school district does not permit research with comparison groups, the writer, following a suggestion of MacGinitie et al. (2000c), utilized the Gates-MacGinitie Reading Tests' norming group as an alternate comparison group. The study group, as a whole, achieved larger-than-expected percentile rank increases from pretest to posttest. Also, five of eight subgroups realized performance gains greater than those of peers in the norming group. Finally, a number of individual students increased in percentile rank beyond what was expected based on comparisons with the norming group.

The determination of whether the group and subgroups realized statistically significant and educationally important achievement results was ascertained in a clear-cut manner by employing this dissertation study's statistical tests. However, determining the effect of the intervention on outcomes in the one-group study was problematic. This concern, as well as an implication of the findings as a whole, is discussed in the next section. The chapter then concludes with a discussion of the study's limitations and recommendations for practice and future research.

Implications of Findings

The research question was answered by the study's findings. The interpretation of findings begins with the results bearing on statistical significance and educational meaningfulness of observed increases in performance. The total group, with a 2.0 mean raw score gain from pretest to posttest, realized statistically significant and educationally important results. The female, White American, and White American female subgroups also secured statistically significant gains in reading comprehension achievement. The same subgroups, the White American males and the African American females, secured educationally meaningful increases in performance. The male, African American male, and African American subgroups did not attain statistically or educationally significant performance outcomes.

The difficulty of definitively ascertaining the impact of an intervention on performance outcomes in a one-group pretest-posttest study has been repeatedly discussed in this document. The writer, nevertheless, believes that a careful consideration of statistical significance, educationally important, and study group-norming group comparison results may lead to informed judgments about the impact of the reading instruction in this dissertation's study on the observed gains in achievement.

NCE scores are percentile ranks statistically transformed into equal interval units of reading achievement that describe a student's or group's level of performance relative to the performance of the standardized test's norming group (MacGinitie et al., 2000c). As previously detailed, MacGinitie et al. (2000c) established criteria for determining whether students and groups most likely realized consequentially larger-than-expected gains in reading achievement from pretest to posttest. In an effort to avoid overstating conclusions, the writer doubled the standards suggested by MacGinitie et al. (2000c). The writer defined the difference score criteria for evaluating the performance of the study's participants relative to the performance of the norming group at 8.0 NCEs (8.0 percentiles) for individual scores and 4.4 NCEs (4.4 percentiles) for group mean scores.

The study group as a whole (difference score = 6.41), females (9.25), White Americans (8.75), White American females (10.80), White American males (5.33), and African American females (4.50); exceeded the 4.4 mean percentile increase criteria. In addition, eight students surpassed the 8.0 standard with gains of between eleven and twenty-nine percentiles. The writer believes that it can be reasonably concluded that the treatment impacted the performance of the group as a whole and of the subgroups and students who achieved large percentile increases. The finding that the total group and five subgroups achieved statistically significant or educationally meaningful increases in reading comprehension achievement supports this judgment.

Two observations may serve to advance a more thorough interpretation of the findings by placing the results in the context of a portion of the high school strategic reading literature. First, the findings suggest that the group, as a whole, benefited from the strategic reading intervention.

Second, the results suggest that the intervention differentially impacted the performances of racial and gender subgroups.

The goal of this applied dissertation was to contribute to the amelioration of a high school's reading achievement concern. The research study involved piloting a strategic reading process that, if successful, could encourage widespread reading instruction in content-area classes at the school. A secondary goal was to contribute to the literature on high school strategic reading programming. To the extent that the findings of this dissertation's study may be judged as indicating an overall positive impact of the intervention on the levels of reading achievement, the study is consistent with and contributes to the literature on the general effectiveness of reading instruction at the secondary level (Alfassi 2004, Brozo and Hargis 2003, Bryant 2003, Frey et al. 2005, Fisher 2001, Myers and Savage 2005, Ogle 1986, Slater and Horstman 2002, Smith and Tompkins 1988, Vacca and Vacca 2002).

The finding that suggests that the reading strategies instruction had differential impact on the performances of racial and gender subgroups is consistent with much of the literature on secondary reading instruction. White American females realized the largest mean percentile increases from pretest to posttest and had the largest effect measure that indicates the educational importance of the increase in performance. Females, as a group, were second in percentile increase and the effect size measure. The White American subgroup was next on both measures of increased achievement. The two African American female participants and the White American male subgroup attained large effect size measures establishing the practical importance of their achievement gains.

The African American male subgroup decreased in mean percentile rank from pretest to posttest. The reported findings are consistent with a large volume of research that indicates higher levels of reading achievement progress are typically attained by female and White American students compared with the overall gains most often realized by male and African American pupils (Allen, Donoghue, and Schoeps 1998; Banks and McGee Banks 2004, Donahue et al. 1999, Fisher 2001, Matczynski et al. 2000, Parsons 2004, Reglin 1995).

Three sets of individual scores were interpreted. These scores significantly affected the overall findings. The writer viewed these sets of scores as indicators of unanticipated performance events. The data from three subgroups indicate achievement gains beyond the writer's expectations, a finding that contrasts with the research found in the literature and a disappointing outcome.

First, three students in the White American female subgroup elevated their pretest percentile scores from the fiftieth percentile range to the seventieth and eightieth ranges on the posttest. The three students achieved nineteen, twenty-one, and twenty-nine percentile rank increases respectively. The writer was confident in concluding that the strategic reading intervention had some influence on the very large performance gains.

Second, in contrast to the overall findings in the literature (Allen et al. 1998, Donahue et al. 1999, Parsons 2004), the White American male subgroup outperformed the White American female subgroup in mean raw score and mean percentile rank. Two of the six students in the group scored at the ninety-ninth percentile on both the pretest and posttest. Two other young men secured moderate increases of one and five percentiles. The remaining members of the subgroup realized, on the basis of the standard established in the data analysis plan, large increases of eleven and fifteen percentiles.

As reported previously, White American females in the study achieved a higher mean percentile gain than any other subgroup in the study.

The White American males, however, realized the highest pretest and posttest mean percentile scores of 75.17 and 80.50 respectively. The White American female group was next with pretest and posttest mean percentile scores of 65.30 and 76.10. Although this finding contradicts the overall results found in the research literature, the writer believes that the finding of superior White American male achievement cannot be used to draw inferences beyond this study. The small group size and the atypical composition of the group, with 33 percent of the members at the ninety-ninth percentile in achievement, make inferences to other populations questionable.

Third, the results bearing on the African American male subgroup are disappointing to the writer. Long before the terms *multicultural education* and *ethic of care* were coined, the writer practiced the principles of the educational approach and of the ethical position. During the intervention phase of the research project, the writer diligently maintained the inclusively welcoming classroom climate and warm rapport that created the conditions to provide equally for the social and emotional needs of all. The strategic reading instruction was multidimensional and the reading selections included many of multicultural content. Finally, the writer held and communicated high expectations for each student.

In spite of the writer's best efforts, the African American male subgroup, as a whole, achieved at a lower level on the posttest than on the pretest. Only two students in the total study group achieved at markedly lower levels from pretest to posttest. Both of these students, with seven percentile rank declines, were in this subgroup. Conversely, the two other young men in the group attained positive results. The first young man achieved a relatively high increase of seven percentiles. The remaining student maintained a good percentile rank of seventy from pretest to posttest.

The concern centered on the failure of the intervention to positively impact on the measured performance of the African American male subgroup anticipates the recommendations for practice and future research. The writer's suggestions follow a report of the study's limitations.

Limitations of the Study

The research study was limited by conditions determined by the school's scheduling procedure and research policy. The instructional day consists of four eighty-minute blocks of time and one forty-minute period. The writer's psychology class was scheduled for the first term of the school year during one of the eighty-minute blocks.

Because the policy of the high school where the study took place does not allow for research entailing differential instruction to test and comparison groups of students, the writer designed and implemented a one-group pretest-posttest study. Threats to the internal validity of a one-group study are present. When extraneous variables, such as maturation, are not controlled by the presence of a comparison group, the ability to determine the effect of a treatment on the observed outcomes is called into question (Gall et al. 2003).

The writer detailed provisions to control for the extraneous variables throughout the data analysis plan and results portions of applied dissertation. The utilization of the standardized test's norming group as a substitute comparison group and the establishment of demanding criteria to evaluate percentile rank increases that may count for evidence of the intervention's impact on outcomes were highlighted. Nevertheless, in the absence of a comparison group of peers from the same school, the writer has very cautiously drawn inferences regarding the possible impact of the strategic reading instruction on the observed gains in achievement. Finally, many of the study's subgroups were small. Care must be exercised in drawing inferences from the findings regarding these groups to populations outside the study.

Recommendations

The writer concludes this paper with three recommendations. One is directed to the school district officials who graciously encouraged this applied dissertation research. The other suggestions are directed to the research community devoted to fostering the growth of each student who educators are privileged and entrusted to serve.

First, the writer believes that the analysis and interpretation of the data collected in the study revealed findings that support a conclusion that the intervention was effective in fostering the increased reading achievement of the study group as a whole, a number of subgroups, and numerous individual students. While vigilantly guarding against overstating the findings, the writer intends to attempt to persuade the high school principal and district superintendent to encourage the high school's teachers to consistently require students to employ strategic reading techniques.

The writer further plans to offer the strategic reading process implemented in the study as a beginning point in discussions among interested professions to determine how strategic reading practices might best be integrated into content-area classes schoolwide. Finally, the writer aims to collaborate with district reading specialists in providing instruction to the high school teaching staff on the rationale for and use of reading strategies in content-area classes.

Second, the writer recommends that future research on high school reading instruction should center on school-wide interventions. The study by Fisher (2001) may serve to inspire and direct future researchers. The writer attained an intuitive sense of the potential benefit of schoolwide reading initiatives by studying the research of Fisher and through this applied dissertation process. Additional research is, however, required to provide the data necessary to embolden leaders in education to confidently promote strategic reading initiatives that span the curricula of high schools.

Third, the writer strongly encourages research focused on planning and delivering instruction to preservice teachers and to professional educators on the principles and practices of multicultural education. The writer's hope is that increasing numbers of professionals will come to a heightened awareness of the duty to acquire the competencies and attitudes necessary to provide well for all students. The writer's vision is of legions of teachers experiencing the elevated interior life that arises from the daily effort to embrace the aspirations of and nurture the growth of every learner.

REFERENCES

Alexander, P. A., and T. L. Jetton (2000). "Learning from Text: A Multidimensional and Developmental Perspective." In *Handbook of Reading Research: Volume III*, edited by M. L. Kamil, P. B. Mosenthal, P. D. Pearson, and R. Barr, 269–284. Hillsdale, NJ: Erlbaum.

Alfassi, M. "Reading to Learn: Effects of Combined Strategy Instruction on High School Students." *The Journal of Educational Research* 97, no. 4 (2004): 171–184.

Allen, N. L., J. R. Donoghue, and T. L. Schoeps. *National Assessment of Educational Progress*. Washington, DC: National Center for Education Statistics, 1998.

American Educational Research Association, American Psychological Association, and National Council of Measurement in Education. *Standards for Educational and Psychological Testing*. Washington, DC: Author, 1999.

Banks, J. A., and C. A. McGee Banks. *Multicultural Education: Issues and Perspectives* (5th ed.). Hoboken, NJ: John Wiley and Sons, 2004.

Bean, T. W. "Reading in the Content Areas: Social Constructivists Dimensions." In *Handbook of Reading Research: Volume III*, edited by M. L. Kamil, P. P. Mosenthal, P. D. Pearson, and R. Barr, 629–644. Hillsdale, NJ: Erlbaum, 2000.

Berk, L. E. *Infants, Children, and Adolescents* (4th ed.). Boston: Allyn and Bacon, 2002.

Brozo, W. G., and C. H. Hargis. "Taking Seriously the Idea of Reform: One High School's Effort to Make Reading More Responsive to All Students." *Journal of Adolescent and Adult Literacy* 47(2003): 14–23.

Bryant, D. P. "Promoting Effective Instruction for Struggling Secondary Students: Introduction to the Special Issue." *Learning Disability Quarterly* 26 (2003): 70–71.

Bryant, D. P., N. Ugel, S. Thompson, and A. Hamff. "Instructional Strategies for Content-Area Reading Instruction." *Intervention in School and Clinic* 34 (1999): 293–304.

Case, R. "The Development of Conceptual Structures." In *Handbook of Child Psychology: Cognition, Perception, and Language*, edited by D. Kuhn and S. Sigler, 745–800. New York: Wiley, 1998.

Collinson, V. "Redefining Teacher Excellence." *Theory into Practice* 38, no. 1 (1999): 4–11.

Day-Vines, N. L. "Ethics, Power, and Privilege: Salient Issues in the Development of Multicultural Competencies for Teachers Serving African American Children with Disabilities." *Teacher Education and Special Education* 23, no. 1 (2000): 3–18.

Derry, S. J. "Cognitive Schema Theory in the Constructivist Debate." *Educational Psychologists* 31, no. 3/4 (1996): 163–174.

Donahue, P. L., K. E. Voelkl, J. R. Campbell, and J. Mazzeo. *The NAEP 1998 Reading Report Card for the Nation and the States* (NCES 1999–500). Washington, DC: U.S. Department of Education, Office of Educational Research and Improvement, National Center for Education Statistics, 1999.

Fisher, D. "We're Moving Up: Creating a Schoolwide Literacy Effort in an Urban High School." *Journal of Adolescent and Adult Literacy* 45 (2001): 92–101.

Frey, B. B., S. W. Lee, N. Tallefson, L. Pass, and D. Massengill. "Balanced Literacy in an Urban School District." *Journal of Educational Research* 98, no. 5 (2005): 272–280.

Gall, M. D., J. P. Gall, and W. R. Borg. *Educational Research: An Introduction* (7th ed.). Boston: Pearson Education Inc., 2003.

Joel, C. "What Makes Literacy Tutoring Effective?" *High School Journal* 83, no. 3 (1996): 10–16.

Johns Hopkins University. *The Talent Development High School with Career Academies*. Baltimore: Author, 1994.

Johns, J. L., and S. D. Lenski. *Improving Reading: Strategies and Resources* (3rd ed.). Dubuque, IA: Kendall/Hunt, 2001.

Kea, C. D., and C. A. Utley. To Teach Me Is to Know Me. *Journal of Special Education* 32, no. 1 (1998): 44–47.

MacGinitie, W. H., R. K. MacGinitie, K. Maria, and L. G. Dreyer. *Gates-MacGinitie Reading Tests* (4th ed.). Itasco, IL: Riverside, 2000a.

MacGinitie, W. H., R. K. MacGinitie, K. Maria, and L. G. Dreyer. *Gates-MacGinitie Reading Tests (Levels 7/9, 10/12): Directions for Administration* (4th ed.). Itasco. IL: Riverside, 2000b.

MacGinitie, W. H., R. K. MacGinitie, K. Maria, and L. G. Dreyer. *Gates-MacGinitie Reading Tests: Manual for Scoring and Interpreting* (4th ed.). Itasco, IL: Riverside, 2000c.

MacGinitie, W. H., R. K. MacGinitie, K. Maria, and L. G. Dreyer. *Gates-MacGinitie Reading Tests: Technical Report* (4th ed.). Itasco, IL: Riverside, 2002.

Matczynski, T. J., J. F. Rogus, T. J. Lasley II, and E. A. Joseph. "Culturally Relevant Instruction: Using Traditional and Progressive Strategies in Urban Schools." *The Educational Forum* 64 (2000): 350–357.

Mayer, R. E. "Learners as Information Processors: Legacies and Limitations of Educational Psychology's Second Metaphor." *Educational Psychologists* 3, no. 3/4 (1996): 151–161.

McCombs, B., and M. L. Barton. "Motivating Secondary School Students to Read Their Textbooks." *NASSP Bulletin,* 82, no. 600 (1998): 24–33.

Myers, M. P., and T. Savage. "Enhancing Student Comprehension of Social Studies Material." *The Social Studies* 96, no. 1 (2005): 18–23.

Newson, J., and E. Newson. "Intersubjectivity and the Transmission of Culture: On the Social Origins of Symbolic Functioning." *Bulletin of the British Psychological Society* 28 (1975): 437–446.

Ogle, D. M. "K-W-L: A Teaching Model that Develops Active Reading of Expository Text." *The Reading Teacher* 39 (1986): 564–570.

Palinscar, A., and A. Brown. "Reciprocal Teaching of Comprehension-Fostering and Comprehension-Monitoring Activities." *Cognition and Instruction 1*, no. 1 (1984): 117–175.

Parsons, L. "Challenging the Gender Divide: Improving Literacy for All." *Teacher Librarian* 32, no. 2 (2004): 8–11.

Quiocho, A. "The Quest to Comprehend Expository Text: Applied Classroom Research." *Journal of Adolescent and Adult Literacy* 40 (1997): 450–455.

Reglin, G. *Achievement for African American Students: Strategies for the Diverse Classroom*. Bloomington, IN: National Educational Service, 1995.

Riley, R. "Improving the Reading and Writing Skills of America's Students." *Learning Disability Quarterly* 1 (1996): 67–69.

Salvia, J., and J. E. Ysseldyke. *Assessment in Special and Inclusive Education* (9th ed.). Boston: Houghton Mifflin, 2004.

Schmidt, R. J., M. S. Rozendal, and G. G. Greenman. "Reading Instruction in the Inclusion Classroom: Research-Based Practices." *Remedial and Special Education* 23 (2002): 130–140.

Semel, E. M., and E. H. Wiig. "Semel Auditory Processing Program: Training Effects among Children with Language-Learning Disabilities." *Journal of Learning Disabilities* 4 (1981): 192–196.

Shaw, A. H., T. M. Roe, and N. Legters. *Strategic Reading: A Resource Guide for Secondary Teachers*. Baltimore: Johns Hopkins University, 2000.

Slater, W. H., and F. R. Horstman. "Teaching Reading and Writing Skills to Struggling Middle School and High School Students: The Case for Reciprocal Teaching." *Preventing School Failure* 46, no. 4 (2002): 163–166.

Smith, P., and G. Tompkins. "Structured Notetaking: A New Strategy for Content Area Readers." *Journal of Reading,* 32, no. 1 (1988): 46–53.

Stevens, L. P. "South Park and Society: Instructional and Curricular Implications of Popular Culture in the Classroom." *Journal of Adolescent and Adult Literacy* 44 (2001): 548–555.

Troy, J. F. "The Myth of Our Failed Educational System." *Ohio Schools* 77, no. 2 (1999): 20–21.

Turnbull, A. P., and H. R. Turnbull. *Families, Professionals, and Exceptionality: Collaborating for Empowerment* (4th ed.). Upper Saddle River, NJ: Prentice Hall, 2001.

United States Department of Labor. *Work force 2000*. Washington, DC: U.S. Government Printing Office, 1998.

Vacca, R. T., and J. A. Vacca. *Content Area Reading: Literacy and Learning across the Curriculum* (7th ed.). Boston: Allyn and Bacon, 2002.

Wilder, M. "Culture, Race, and Schooling: Toward a Non-Color-Blind Ethic of Care." *The Education Forum* 63 (1999): 356–362.

APPENDIX A

BDA Chart

BDA

Before 　　My Knowledge	My Questions
During 　　Answers to Questions	Notes

DR. DONALD J. YOKITIS

After 　　My Choice (Check) _____ Structured Notes _____ Written Summary	_____ Research and Present _____ Concept Mapping	
Name-_____ Date-_____	Subject-_____ Pages-_____	Strategy (B-D-A)

APPENDIX B

Concept Mapping

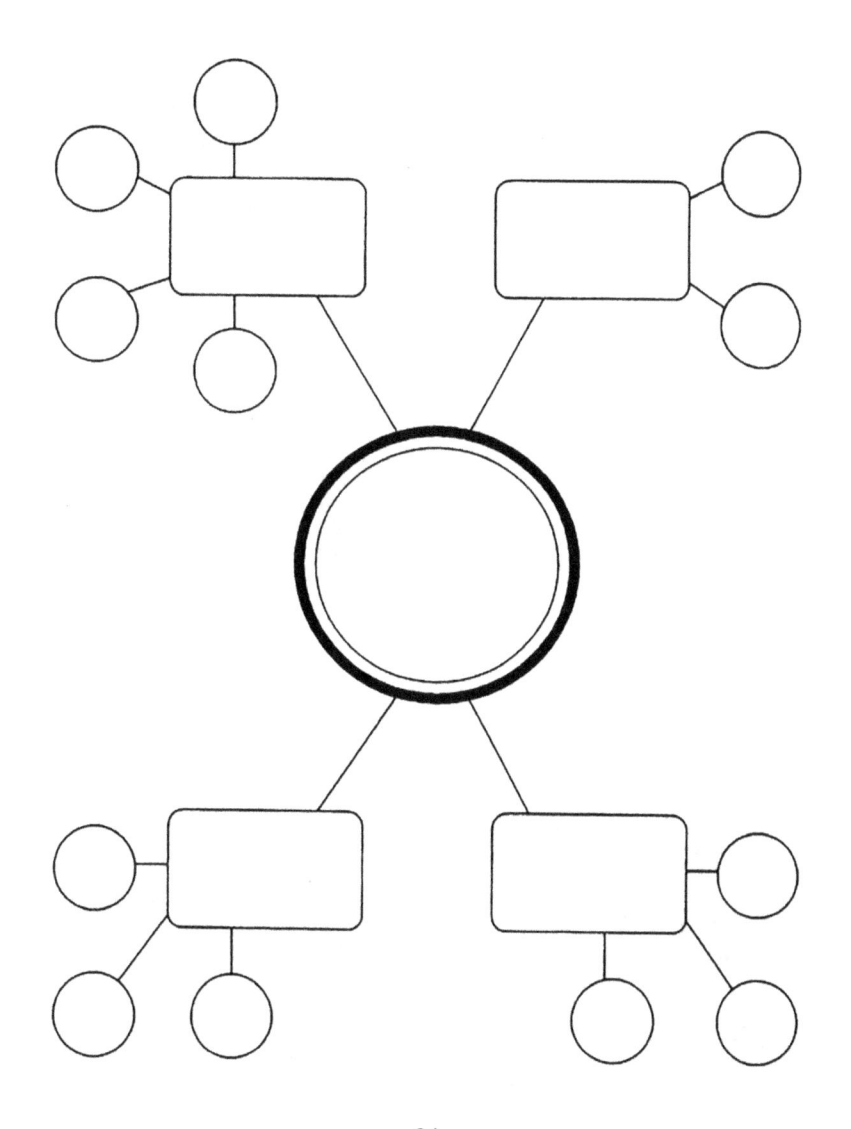

APPENDIX C

Structures Notes

I.
    A.
        1.
            a.
            b.
            c.
        2.
            a.
            b.
            c.
        3.
            a.
            b.
            c.
    B.
        1.
        2.
        3.
    C.
        1.
        2.
        3.

II.
    A.
    B.
    C.

III.
    A.
    B.
    C.

ABOUT THE AUTHOR

Donald Yokitis has been a serious student for over fifty years and a teacher-professor for over forty-six years. His formal education includes earning a bachelor's degree in elementary education from Slippery Rock University in Pennsylvania, a master's degree in special education from Shippensburg University in Pennsylvania, a social studies certificate from Saint Francis University in Pennsylvania, and a doctor of education degree from Nova Southern University in Davie, Florida.

Donald Yokitis has taught students in general education and in special education in grades one to twelve. On a part-time basis, he has taught at the undergraduate and graduate levels. Finally, Donald Yokitis continues to tutor high school and elementary-age students.

Recently, Donald Yokitis has published *A Caring Errand: A Handbook for Educators, Future Educators and Students' Caregivers,* which can be purchased from Amazon, Barnes and Noble, Target, iTunes, or Google Play.

Donald Yokitis and his wife, Sue, reside in Nanty-Glo, Pennsylvania. They are the parents of three young adults and the grandparents of two young children.

CPSIA information can be obtained
at www.ICGtesting.com
Printed in the USA
BVHW010548210322
631597BV00005B/60